Table of Coi

Backlash

Frank & Stein
Murder Mystery

Kerry Costello

KERRY COSTELLO
BOOKS

"The forces of retribution are always listening. They never sleep."
Meg Greenfield

---

1. https://youtu.be/u7plOZDOB7Ac;%20kerry@kerrycostellobooks.com
2. https://youtu.be/u7plOZDOB7Ae;%20kerry@kerrycostellobooks.com

CHAPTER 1

Naples Florida

The Uber dropped him off on Third Street. He walked up the steps of the mall and towards the shop, stopping briefly to close his eyes and take a deep breath of the fresh sea air. He suddenly realized how much he would miss Naples when they moved on. *Got to give some serious thought to buying a place here*, he thought as he unlocked the shop door. Closing the door behind him, he wandered around aimlessly, then went into the back room. The clothes rail caught his eye.

He walked over and smiled as he examined the costumes. Taking one of his favorite jackets off the rail, he put it on and admired himself in the full-length mirror. The front door opened and a voice he recognized shouted.

"Hello anyone here?" He took the jacket off, put it back on the coat hanger.

"Yeah, in here," he shouted as he hung the jacket back up on the clothes rail. The visitor walked into the room.

"Hey," said the visitor.

"Hey yourself," said the man.

"Do you know what time the others are getting here?" said the visitor. The man looked at his watch.

"They were due in about forty-five minutes, but they called earlier to say they're running a little late."

"What's new?" said the visitor.

"Yeah. They said the new security guys should arrive about the same time." The visitor smiled.

"Okay, so enough time to talk."

"Sure. So, what was it you wanted to talk to me about?"

CHAPTER 2

Frankie parked his silver Jeep Cherokee on Third Street Old Naples and stepped out into the pleasant heat of an October Florida morning. He looked around... *busy busy as usual.* Frankie James Armstrong stood a little under six feet tall, had a wiry physique, salt and pepper hair and a slightly crooked nose, courtesy of a drunken fight he'd had with a fellow soldier back in his army days.

Third Street Naples is just two blocks from the historic 19th Century Naples Pier and a stone's throw from the Gulf of Mexico's glorious beaches. The street is surrounded by original colorful beach cottages and the beautiful grand houses of Old Naples. Designer shops line the main thoroughfare, alongside 'fine dining' restaurants and chic bistros. Courtyards and fountains nestle amidst the lush colorful flowers cascading from hanging baskets dangling from the antique streetlights of historic Third Street South.

Looking across the street, Frankie saw his partner Sam Randazzo, already waiting on the sidewalk near the corner of Thirteenth and Third. Sam stood out from the tourists with his slim physique, fine Mediterranean features, dark hair, and was as usual, smartly dressed. Today it was a light beige linen suit, white shirt and blue tie. Randazzo didn't do casual when he was on business. Frankie was dressed in shorts, a light blue T-shirt and a white linen shirt. He couldn't remember the last time he'd worn a tie.

Sam Randazzo and Frankie Armstrong had recently formed a private security and investigations firm - F&S Investigations and Security. Global Pictures was their first client. They'd been hired on a recommendation from the Naples Police department. Global Pictures needed to hire security while they filmed their movie, and in particular, personal security for their star actor Ricky Jordan.

Clive Susman, the movie director, had explained to Sam that the company planned to film several scenes in and around Naples and the nearby Everglades. The scenes were for Ricky Jordan's next movie, with the working title 'Backlash'. The film crew and cast were all staying at The Inn on Fifth, but Susman wanted a base near to Third Street and Naples Pier where a lot of scenes were to be shot.

Global had rented a shop in the abandoned mall in Old Naples for the duration of the filming. The mall owners were waiting for permission from the city to demolish it and build a hotel on the site. In the meantime, they were renting out empty shops on short-term leases. It was strategically ideal as a temporary location for the movie company, who needed a base for meetings, makeup, props, storage of actor's clothes, film equipment and such.

Clive Susman had arranged to meet Sam Randazzo and his partner at the shop, so he could introduce them to the Executive producer, the crew and movie star Ricky Jordan.

Sam spotted Frankie and waved. He waved back and crossed the road.

"Morning Frankie."

"Morning, Sam," said Frankie, looking at his watch. "Are we on time?"

"We're actually an hour early now. I got a text earlier from this Susman guy to say he needed to reschedule the meeting for 11:00 a.m. But I'd already agreed to drop Martha off at the school, so here I am. I thought you could buy me a coffee. We could use the time to plan how we get more clients. As it stands, this is our one and only job."

"Okay, suits me. Where exactly is the meeting?"

"A shop in the abandoned mall. Maybe we should go see where this shop is first? I've got the address right here," he said, taking out his cell phone and scrolling through his messages. "Here it is."

They walked up Third, past Tommy Bahamas, Sea Salt, then turned left into the mall and found the empty unit.

"This looks like the place," said Frankie, walking over to the shop window, putting his hand up to shield the glare to look inside.

"No one there yet, I guess," said Sam.

"Doesn't look like it. No lights on."

"Come on, let's go for that coffee."

"Okay," said Frankie, moving away from the window and going to the shop door. He twisted the handle. The door opened. Sam raised his eyebrows.

"You'd think it'd be locked."

"You would," said Frankie, opening the door wide and waving Sam in, like a flunky at a swanky hotel.

"You know what they say about curiosity?"

"Essential to being a detective?" Frankie replied, smiling.

"Yeah, okay, smart ass. Let's have a look inside." They went in.

"Hello, anyone here?" said Frankie in a loud voice. There was no answer. They looked at each other, both sensing something intangible. "Let's look in back," said Frankie. They walked through an archway in the dividing wall and into a spacious rear storage area. On the right-hand side of the room, a large clothes rail lay on its side, clothes strewn over the floor. They walked around the fallen rail and stopped.

"What the hell...," said Frankie. The body of a man lay on the floor, head to one side, a small hole visible in the side of his temple. Blood had seeped from the wound and stained the wooden floor. A folded piece of paper lay on top of the body.

Sam Randazzo walked over, kneeled down to check for a pulse, turned, looked up at his partner, and shook his head slightly. He looked more closely at the wound.

"Looks like a .22 caliber," Sam said and stood up.

"So, maybe someone he knew?" said Frankie

"To get that close, and with little sign of a struggle?" Sam shrugged, "probably." Frankie bent down and twisted his head to get a good look at the victim's face.

"Jesus Christ almighty! Unless I'm very much mistaken, this is Ricky Jordan. Well, was Ricky Jordan. Never seen him in real life, but...."

"What?!" said Sam, now taking a good look at the man's face. "Holy mother of God!" muttered Randazzo, taking out his cell phone. He punched in a number.

"Better check the rest of this place out Frankie." Frankie nodded, took his gun out of its holster and went to check out the rest of the shop. It didn't take long. There were two large cupboards in front which were empty and a wooden staircase leading to a top floor, which comprised one large empty open space. *Presumably used as a stock room when it was a working shop,* thought Frankie as he made his way back downstairs. Sam's call was answered. "Hello, yeah, put me through to Captain Alex Reagan please, it's urgent, yes Sam Randazzo, I'll hold." While they waited, Frankie looked down at the corpse again.

"Our first assignment and we find our client shot dead. Is this how it's going to be?"

"Some start for sure," said Sam. "Baptism by fire, Frankie boy." Sam turned his attention back to his cellphone. "Hello Alex, Sam Randazzo. Yeah, I know, only been gone five minutes and I'm calling you already. No, I'm not missing you," Sam said, responding to the obvious jibe. "Yes, I do know what they call us down there. That's old news, Alex. Look, this is serious. We're on our first assignment, looking after a film star guy, Ricky Jordan. Yeah, that Ricky Jordan."

"How so? One of your guys recommended us. Jordan's on location down here in southwest Florida. Look, the thing is, we've just found him dead. Shot in the head, with a .22 from the looks of it. Yes, seriously. Would I pull your leg about something like this? Yeah, well, that was different. Anyway, this is serious. I'd have called 911, but I thought you might want a heads' up first, seeing as how it's going to attract a lot of publicity. No, no one else knows yet, not even the guy who hired us, the Director Clive Susman. He and his film crew are due here shortly."

"Where? we're in one of the empty shops in the abandoned mall behind Third Street in Old Naples. Call me when you're on Third and I'll come out to get you. Will you alert the CSI guys, or do you want me to call 911? No, okay, I'll leave that with you. No, I won't mess the crime scene up. No, I will not let the film crew in. You think I've suddenly turned into an amateur now I'm private? Yeah okay." Randazzo cut the line and looked at Frankie.

"I got that," said Frankie. "Do we call Susman, or do we wait?" Randazzo took out a pair of plastic gloves and pulled them on.

"We wait, but don't let them in. First, we have a little peek at that note," and he walked carefully over to where the body lay, kneeled down, picked up the note and unfolded it. "Okay Frankie, get your cell, take a close-up of the note, then video the entire scene. Be quick." Frankie did as Randazzo asked. Randazzo folded the note back up and placed it back on the body. "You finished?" Frankie nodded. "Okay, let's go wait outside."

While they waited, Frankie looked at his cell and the picture of the note he'd photographed.

"What do you make of it?" said Frankie, showing Sam the picture of the note on his cell phone. *'You messed with the wrong people'* "Not much of a clue, is it?"

"Well, maybe it is," said Sam. "See, it seems odd to me. This is the sort of note you'd leave after you've beaten someone up. You know, a warning not to carry on doing what you've been doing. I don't see the point of leaving that sort of note on the person you just killed."

"So why leave a note at all?"

"An amateur might want to throw someone off the scent. Make it look like some sort of revenge killing. I don't know, it just doesn't feel right."

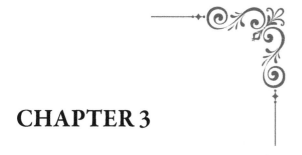

CHAPTER 3

The captain called Sam when he was on Third. Randazzo went to get him and brought him to the shop. Sam made the introductions. The captain had brought along a colleague.

"This is my partner in crime, Frankie Armstrong," said Randazzo, "Frankie, meet Captain Alex Reagan and Lieutenant Detective Dale Vogel. Dale's my replacement in the department." Frankie shook hands with both men.... *Did I detect a bit of tension between Sam and Dale?* thought Frankie. Both the captain and the detective donned plastic gloves and put overshoes on.

"Okay, show me," said the captain. Sam led them further into the shop and to the scene of the crime. Reagan and Vogel stopped, looked around, and took it all in. Vogel took out a notepad and pen, peered around studiously at the floor, the walls and ceiling, then made some notes. "Right, seen enough," said the captain. "Let's leave now so we don't contaminate the scene any more than we have to." Sam led them all back outside.

To one side of the small, enclosed mall, there were a few chairs scattered around an old metal table outside an abandoned café. Captain Reagan walked over to the table, looked at the chairs and signaled to them all to sit down. Once they were seated, the captain spoke.

"So, fill me in on this assignment, Sam. From the beginning."

"Okay. Well, we, sorry I, got a call from sergeant Andrews, Bill Andrews. He's..."

"Yeah, I know him," said Reagan.

"Bill said they'd had an enquiry about the possibility of providing some sort of protection or security for a movie star. A guy called Clive Susman, the movie director, said they're down here filming some scenes with Ricky Jordan in our neck of the woods. His new movie's called Backlash. Said they'd chosen Naples to shoot some scenes on Third, some daring stunts off the pier, that sort of thing. Then off to the Everglades, then Miami."

"So, Andrews tells him it's not a police matter and suggests he hires some private security. Andrews remembered us and recommended the guy contacts me and...." Sam shrugged.

"Okay, so did you meet with this Susman guy?"

"No, it was all done by phone. We're scheduled to meet Susman and the rest of the crew this morning, here at the shop at 11:00 a.m. They've rented this place to use as a temporary base for props, meetings and such while they're down here. They're due here any time," said Randazzo, looking at this watch. "In fact, I think this is them now."

They all turned to look in the direction Sam was looking. A group of three men and one woman were walking purposefully across the square towards the shop. The captain stood up.

"We'd better go tell them what's happened. Sam, you and Frankie take the lead on this. It's your client, and you two found the body, so..."

"Okay Cap," said Sam. And they all got up and walked towards the little group of visitors to intercept them. Frankie stopped suddenly and tugged at Sam's arm. "What the hell.... that's Ricky Jordan!" he said.

They all stopped.

"What in the blazes is going on, Sam?" said the captain. "You said the body in there was Ricky Jordan. So, was it him or not?" Sam was shaking his head.

"You saw the body in there, Alex."

"I did, but I wouldn't know this Ricky Jordan character if he jumped out and bit me."

"Wait here," said Sam. Frankie, you come with me." And the two of them approached the small group.

"Which of you is Clive Susman?" asked Sam.

"I'm Clive Susman," said the man on the left. He was medium height, dressed in jeans, T-shirt and sported a red New York Yankees cap, peak pulled down, framing his whiskery face. "You're the security guys, I assume?"

"Yes. I'm Sam Randazzo. We've spoken on the phone. This is my partner, Frankie Armstrong."

"Okay," said Susman, "well nice to meet you in the flesh." He shook hands with Sam and Frankie. "So, shall we all go into the shop and get down to business?"

"Sorry, we can't. There's been a..., a development."

"Development? What kind of development? And who are those people?" Susman said, pointing at the captain and Vogel.

"That's Captain Alex Reagan and Detective Dale Vogel of the Naples Police department."

"Naples police department? What in the hell is going on here?" he said, clearly annoyed and confused. The other three members of the group looked equally perplexed.

"We found a body. In the shop," said Sam. "We were early, and the door was open, so we went in and found the body of a man. Someone had shot him."

"What?! What man?" said the woman, clearly horrified.

"Well, we thought... well, up until now, we assumed it was Ricky Jordan, but..." Sam looked at the man on right who looked exactly like Ricky Jordan.

"Oh my God," said the woman, "Billy, it must be Billy."

"Forgive me," said Sam, "but who's Billy?"

CHAPTER 4

The woman looked close to collapse, so Sam suggested they all go over and sit at the table. There weren't enough chairs to go round, so Frankie, Sam and Ricky Jordan remained standing. They made introductions all round. Ricky Jordan stood out from the rest, thought Frankie, looking just like the superstar he was. Frankie judged Ricky to be just over six feet tall, with a firm looking athletic physique, fine chiseled features all in proportion. He had slightly tanned skin, perfect white teeth and clear blue eyes. His longish wavy hair was a glossy, mid-brown color. Are these people just born as perfect specimens or do they have to work at it every day? Frankie wondered. Other than Ricky, they all wore lanyard name tags around their necks with titles.

The producer, Ross Sharkey, the shocked but shapely brunette who'd suggested the body was that of someone called Billy, seemed to have now regained her composure and also remained standing. Ricky Jordan stood by her side. Clive Susman, the Director, and Doug Ramsay, the head cameraman, sat down, as did the captain and Dale Vogel.

"So, first off," said Sam, addressing Ross Sharkey, "please explain to us who this Billy is."

"He's... or should I say, he was, Ricky's stunt double. Hence the reason you thought his body was that of Ricky here," she said, nodding in Ricky Jordan's direction. "His name is Billy Fairman. Hasn't been with us that long."

"So, what happened to Billy exactly?" asked Jordan, both hands turned outwards in a questioning manner, "I mean, who the hell would want to shoot him? I can't believe it, just can't...., you said he was shot, yeah? I mean...." he choked out the last couple of words, too emotional to carry on speaking and shaking his head. Ross put her arm around him. He buried his head in her shoulder and wept quietly.

The captain looked up, coughed and asked Randazzo to tell everyone exactly what they'd found when he and Frankie had entered the shop, but they were interrupted by the arrival of the Scene of Crime team. Randazzo looked at the captain.

"Better go let them in, Sam, and explain the situation." Sam walked over, showed the SOC people in and, after a couple of minutes, exited the shop to rejoin the group, who, it seemed, had maintained an awkward silence whilst he was gone. Susman and his colleagues were all looking down at the ground. Ricky Jordan seemed to have recovered his composure some, but Ross still stood by his side.

"Okay, Sam, tell these folks what you found." Sam explained how he and Frankie had arrived at the shop earlier and found the door unlocked. Then described how they'd found a man's body in the back and how they'd immediately informed Captain Reagan at the Naples Police HQ.

"We assumed the body was that of Ricky Jordan, but now it's obvious we jumped to the wrong conclusions. That's pretty well it. Now you know as much as we do," said Sam. The captain spoke next.

"Okay, so Dale here, is going to talk to each of you individually now. Get your contact details, some background on the victim and whatever other relevant information you can provide. We'll need to talk to you again sometime, but after you've spoken to Dale, you're free to go." They all nodded. "Okay," the captain continued, "while you're doing that, I'll just have another word with Sam and Frankie here, then Dale and I will be leaving. Thanks for your cooperation so far, and my sympathy for your loss." The captain stood and signaled for Randazzo and Frankie to follow him to the other side of the small mall, away from the group.

"Okay Sam, Frankie, naturally we'll start to investigate this killing. Dale will head up the investigation for the Naples Police department, but if the movie company decide to carry on filming, and if they keep you two on...."

"Yeah, I get it Alex. And yes, we'll keep you informed of anything we find out." The captain looked at Sam.

"Make sure you do. No playing private eye at the expense of the Naples Police Department. Got that Sam?"

"Yeah, I got it the first time. Don't worry." The captain looked as if he was going to add something else but seemed to change his mind. He turned on his heel and walked away.

"What was that all about? I thought you got on well with the captain?" said Frankie.

"I do, but he knows I'm a much better investigator than old Dale. He doesn't want me to upstage him. Wouldn't look good on the Cap, would it?"

"I guess not. Looks like Dale's finished his interviews. Maybe we should go see if we've still got a job."

"Before we do that, I don't know. I guess it's just the detective in me, but quite separate from the security job. I think I have to see if I can find anything more out about this killing. Just walking away and doing nothing just seems, I don't know, wrong somehow. I'm not going to be able to spend a lot of time on it, just some initial poking around."

"I understand. And if it's okay with you, I'll tag along. I'm not exactly over busy, so as long as I get some time to go fishing, I'd be up for helping out."

"Deal. Gives me a chance to teach you some more sleuthing tips and tricks." Frankie laughed.

"How could I resist?"

Ricky Jordan was still looking grim as they walked back to the Global Pictures movie people. Clive Susman and Ross Sharkey seemed to be having a heated exchange but stopped talking as Sam and Frankie came near. Frankie spoke.

"This may not be the best time to ask, but have you decided if you want us to continue with the security assignment, or are you still deciding whether to continue with your plans? If you need some time to decide, we quite understand, so..." Susman looked at Sharkey, then Susman spoke.

"Yes, we were just discussing that, er, Sam, and I think the consensus is that we carry on. It may take us some time to find a replacement for Billy, but there are plenty of scenes we can shoot with no need for a stunt double, so yes, we wish you and Frankie, isn't it?" Frankie nodded. "We wish you to carry on as arranged."

"Okay, great, that's not a problem, but Frankie and I were just discussing something else. Having found the body, we feel a bit obliged to do some nosing around. See if we can find anything out. It would be in our own time and wouldn't impact on our arrangement with you." Ross Sharkey stepped forward, looking concerned.

"Why would you do that?" she said. "Won't the police be investigating? Won't they resent you..., well interfering?"

"As to the first part of your question, why would I do it? I don't have a good answer, other than I've been a detective most of my adult life and it gets into your blood. We don't intend to stay with it for long, just like I say, ask around a bit, see if we can turn anything up. As for the second part, I don't know if they'll mind but they can't stop me, or should I say stop us." Ross Sharkey nodded.

"I think I understand, er, Sam. Clive told me you were a police detective until a short while ago, so I can see how, as you say, it's in your blood. But maybe I have a better idea. Why don't you look into the killing of Billy, and investigate his murder on our behalf?" Sam looked over at Frankie, who shrugged his shoulders in a 'why not' expression.

"Okay..., well, I guess we could at that." Randazzo said.

"That way you'd be paid for your time, and of course, any reasonable expenses. I would personally like to know who the evil bastard was, who killed Billy. I hadn't got to know him that well, but he seemed like a sweet man."

"Well, I guess the answer is yes. The costs shouldn't be that much, our time and maybe some travel expenses and so on. And as you alluded to before, we'd have to be careful not to step on the captain's toes. It might be better if we kept it confidential for the time being. Captain Reagan has already made it clear to us that if we come across any information which might help his investigation, we should hand that over, so...."

"I think we understand," Ross Sharkey said, looking meaningfully at Susman. He nodded. She turned back to Sam. "Consider yourselves hired to also look into the murder of Billy Fairman on our behalf. You'll need some information on Billy, so call me, but not today. It's too raw. I'll be the person you report to on this aspect of your assignment. Film set security, its Clive, Billy's murder investigation, it's me, clear? If you can't reach me, leave a message. I always check my voicemail."

"Yes ma'am," said Sam. She dug into her purse, brought out a card and handed it to Sam. "All my contact details are on there." Randazzo looked at the card.

"New York?"

"Yes, that's where I'm based, but I'm staying at the Ritz-Carlton while we're down here." Randazzo nodded and pocketed the card. "Catch the bastard who did this," she added with not inconsiderable venom, then turned, walked away out of the mall towards Third Street. The rest of them followed.

"So," Frankie asked Randazzo, "now you've met him, what do you think of our client Ricky Jordan?"

"Not sure. Too soon to judge, really. He's got the presence, sultry look and all, but maybe that's just the circumstances?"

"Yeah, this might be an interesting gig, Sam. Our first assignment and we already have a dead body."

"Look," said Sam, "nothing more to do here today I guess, and I got a few errands to run now, so what says we catch up tomorrow?"

"Yeah, sure. Call me."

CHAPTER 5

BEFORE

Frankie had completely forgotten he'd applied until he opened the official looking brown envelope. He had to read it twice to make sure he understood. He picked up his cell phone to make a call.

"Hey Frankie, you're calling early," said Daisy. "I know you miss me, but this early in the morning?"

"Sorry Daisy, I just had to share my good news."

"What good news Frankie, you've won the lottery or something?"

"Sort of, well not money, but even better, as far as I'm concerned."

"Come on Frankie, I have a face to put on before I expose myself to the world this morning."

"Remember the Green Card lottery? I told you about it when we went to Pepe's last January, or was it February? Anyway, I won one."

"Yes, I remember. So, you're saying you've got a Green Card, they've given you a Green Card. Wow?"

"Yes, I know. It means I can stay here indefinitely, well almost indefinitely. I can get a job, or in my case, probably start a business. Okay, so it's not full American citizenship, but still."

"That's fantastic news, well done. But what about your business back home in the UK?"

"Yeah, I have to think on that. Thing is, I much prefer living here. My divorce will go through soon and Penny gets the house as part of the settlement. So, there's really nothing and nowhere to go back to. There's only the security business to consider. And I think I might be able to do a deal with my partner Derek on that. I've been away so much recently, I'm not sure it'll make that much difference, me being here permanently."

Frankie Armstrong and his business partner, Derek Barns, went back a long way. They lived in the same neighborhood as kids and went to the same school. When they left school, they were both rudderless, and both ended up in dead-end jobs they were less than happy with. They still saw each other socially, mostly in the local pub. During a drunken conversation one night, Derek suggested they join the British Army. The next day, they both joined up, volunteering for the Special Forces Division, and subsequently ended up fighting in the Iraq war in 2003.

Both found their time in the army, and in particular, fighting in a war, a life-changing experience. When they left the forces, they once again found themselves without direction. They'd discussed using their army experience to set up a security company, focusing initially on personal security, but they had no actual idea where and how to start. That was until serendipity intervened. Derek bumped into an old school friend in a pizza parlor who offered them a well-paid job providing personal security for a visiting Arab prince coming to the UK looking at racing stock for his stables back in Saudi Arabia.

It was the lucky break they needed, and on the back of it, they set up A & B Security. They expanded into various areas of the industry, including latterly, IT security, courtesy of Derek's nerdy computer wizard cousin Gareth. That new direction grew the business well beyond their expectations, and they eventually became extremely successful.

"Wow Frankie, this is a lot to take in. Will you stay in your rental in the Acadiana, or buy a place?"

"Haven't really thought that far ahead yet, but I think I'd like to stay here. I love this place, magnificent views over the bay, convenient for the beaches and fishing. Maybe the condo owner would sell my unit to me. Look, I know it's only Wednesday, and we weren't due to go out until Friday, but if you're doing nothing tonight, how about we go to dinner at Cibao and celebrate? Nice slap-up meal. What d'you say?"

"I'd be a misery to say no, Frankie."

"I'll pick you up at 6:30." He put the phone down, smiling. "Come on, Charlie, let's go for a walk." Charlie wagged his tail.

Frankie's cell buzzed just as he was walking out of the condo door. He stopped and answered.

"Sam."

"Frankie, you got a minute."

"Sure, Sam, but let me call you back. Just going out to take Charlie for a walk. I'll call you when we're out on Crayton Road, and I can concentrate. I'm glad you called. I've got news."

"So have I, Call me back." Frankie pocketed his cell, locked the condo door, put Charlie's leash on and walked down the stairs, through the parking lot, and out on to Harbour Drive, heading for their walk around Venetian Bay. Frankie took out his cell and called his friend Sam Randazzo. Sam answered on the second ring.

"Okay, I can speak now, Sam. You want to tell me your news, or shall I go first?"

"You first," said Randazzo, "I get the feeling it's good news."

"I think so, yes. You know how much I enjoy living over here."

"You've made that clear enough for sure, so?"

"Well, I thought my chances of getting a Green Card were slim, but last year I found out about the Green Card Lottery. You apply and they grant a limited number of winners each year. I wasn't sure I qualified, but I entered nevertheless, and I've won. They've granted me a Green Card. Means I can stay, get a job or maybe start a business."

"Congratulations Frankie, that's really great news."

"Thanks Sam. So, what's your news?"

"Not so good. I failed the medical. That bullet I took in the leg back when. They say I gotta retire. Me, Lieutenant Sam Randazzo, the guy who solves more crimes than the rest of 'em put together. Retire... what on earth am I going to do? I can't retire. I don't fish, I don't hunt, I don't paint, don't do woodwork, nothing. Don't do anything like that."

"When?"

"I don't know. I'm waiting to meet with the Chief. See if I can get him to use his influence to get the decision reversed. I know he won't want to lose me, that's for sure."

"That's tough. Can't imagine you not being a detective."

"You and me both Frankie, you and me both. Listen, the main reason I called was to ask you to tell Daisy. She can visit her nephew now. I don't have her number, but if she wants to call me, I can tell her how she can visit. Naturally, everything has to be very tight. The witness protection program is more secure than a nun's knickers."

"Okay, Sam, I'll tell her and get her to call you. Ethan's doing okay, though, is he?"

"I believe he's settled in really well up north. Weather's not too bad up there at this time of the year, but he's gonna get a shock when the real winter weather sets in. A Florida boy all his life, I think, so it's going to take some adjustment."

"I guess so, Sam, but better than being dead. Call me and let me know how you go on with the chief. If he doesn't come through on your request for a reversal, maybe we can start our own detective agency." Sam laughed.

"Yeah, right. I'll call you."

Frankie and Daisy were sitting on one of the two person high top dining tables in their favorite restaurant, The Cibao Grill in Park Shore Plaza. Drinks had been served, food ordered, and now they relaxed, sipping their respective drinks. Daisy had a gin martini straight up with two olives and Frankie had a beer. He passed on Sam's message about being able to visit her brother.

Daisy's brother had flirted with drugs some months previously and unwittingly became involved with a gang of drug dealers. He'd realized his mistake when his good friend was murdered. So he asked Frankie to help. Frankie told him his only way out was to go to his friend Detective Sam Randazzo and tell him the truth and ask if he could help. Eventually, Ethan took Frankie's advice. Sam persuaded Ethan to give evidence, which led to the conviction of the leaders of the drug cartel. In return, Sam subsequently arranged for Ethan to enter the witness protection program.

"That's great news, Frankie. Would you come with me to see Ethan?"

"Yes, of course. Make a weekend of it, maybe?"

"Why not? I'll get some dates organized and let you know. So, you said something in the Uber about Sam Randazzo. He might be retiring. I can't believe that."

"It's true. Not his choice and it's still uncertain, but he sounded worried. That bullet wound in his leg, it's been troubling him ever since it happened."

"So, what was the guy's name, the guy who shot him? A friend of yours wasn't he, Roger Tuckerman, right?"

"Yup, that's the guy. Crazy pants Tuckerman. Shot Sam, then hijacked a plane and took me on a flight I'll never forget. I hated those little planes enough before, but after that experience...."

"Here come the starters," he said, and they both leaned back while the server put down their respective dishes, crab cakes for Frankie, lettuce wedge for Daisy.

"And they never found the guy, Roger Tuckerman?"

"Nope, he ran off. The cops chased him, but he escaped. Last seen climbing a high fence into an alligator farm. The cops decided they'd give up at that point."

"And they left it at that?"

"No, they got the alligator farm owners to check the next day and found nothing other than a shredded gray sneaker, similar to the ones Tuckerman was wearing."

"Jeez," said Daisy.... Frankie shrugged his shoulders.

"Tuck in, Daisy, don't know about you, but I'm starving." They ate for a while, then Daisy spoke.

"So, come on, any ideas about what you're going to do now you can stay and work here an' all?"

"Not really. I've obviously been thinking about possibilities. I wondered about selling my share of A&B security to my partner Derek back in the UK."

"What about income Frankie, could you manage without the income from the company?"

"Yeah, I'm okay for money, even after the cost of my divorce. I'd get a pretty penny for my shares by selling them to Derek, and combined with my investments and my pension, I'd have comfortable retirement money. But hey, I'm far too young to consider retiring. Can't go fishing every day, that would get really boring."

"But would you want to lose contact with the business you helped build?" asked Penny

"No, If Derek agreed, I'd keep back some shares and go on a modest retainer. So, he could continue to have the benefit of my input. I think he'd go for that." Daisy had finished her wedge and drained her martini.

"Another?" asked Frankie.

"Is the Pope a Catholic?" Daisy replied, smiling. Frankie signaled the waiter for more drinks. Another server came and cleared their empty plates away.

"So, in that case, what would you do over here?"

"Haven't got a clue Daisy," said Frankie as their drinks and next course arrived.

CHAPTER 6

Before

Frankie woke, got up and did some stretching exercises on the lanai before putting Charlie on his leash and going out for his usual jog come morning walk for Charlie. There were a few wispy clouds around and a welcome, if brief, sprinkling of rain as they set off around Venetian Bay. The clouds soon cleared, and the day became breezy and sunny. He never tired of Naples and savored every single day.

Frankie spent much of his time on his jog thinking about his options, now he had the treasured Green Card, feeling elated and frustrated in equal measure. He finally had what he'd yearned for and now had no real idea what to do with it. He also had to figure out how to break the news to Derek Barns, his business partner and best friend. Will Derek be thrilled for me or disappointed that I want to stay in Naples?

Frankie jogged on, having several trial conversations in his head with his business partner and trying to figure out what he could do with his new found freedom to live and work in America. He didn't come to any conclusions and decided to put the whole thing out of his mind for the time being.

After breakfast, he sat at his PC to catch up on his emails. Just as he sat down, his cell buzzed Sam.

"Hi Sam, how did your meeting go?"

"You free Frankie? I'd like to drop by later, have a chat."

"Sure, no problem. Everything okay?"

"Yeah, just something I wanted to discuss. Probably better in person than on the phone." Frankie raised his eyebrows, sounds ominous.

"Yeah, no problem, anytime. No particular plans for today, anyway. See you when you get here." Frankie put his cell phone down, and pondered, then shrugged his shoulders and got on with reading his emails. Half an hour later, the doorbell chimed. Charlie rushed to the door, always happy to greet a visitor. Frankie opened the door. Charlie did a little dance to celebrate Sam's arrival, then put his paws up on Randazzo's legs. Randazzo was smartly dressed as usual - lightweight gray jacket, pale blue shirt, burnt orange colored tie and dark blue slacks.

"Hello little feller," said Randazzo, bending down to ruffle Charlie's hair.

"Sit down Sam. I've got some coffee ready." Randazzo took a chair at the dining table. Frankie came out of the kitchen with two coffees, put them on the table, and sat down. Randazzo took a sip, then spoke.

"The meeting wasn't successful, leastways not in the way I'd hoped it might be. Chief Sullivan says he can't go up against the doc. All manner of implications if he did, so..., said he really didn't want to lose me, and I believe him. We've worked together for some years now and always got along." Frankie expressed his sympathy. "However, he did make a suggestion." Randazzo stopped talking and took a sip of his coffee, then looked at Frankie. He seemed to be weighing something up.

"What?" said Frankie

"He suggested I consider working as a PI." Frankie thought for a couple of beats.

"I think that's a great suggestion. You have all the experience any client could wish for. I assume the leg injury wouldn't affect you getting a license to become a PI?"

"No, no problem. Thing is, well, you said the other day, and I appreciate you were probably joking at the time, but you said something about starting our own detective agency. Now before you say anything, just have a think about it, okay? You did say you now have a Green Card and you're free to stay and work in the US. I reckon the chief would be happy enough to help you get a PI license. We've worked together on a couple of cases now, informally I know, but we worked well together, so I thought....?

"But, like I say, don't commit to anything now. Just have a think and if the answer's no, then no hard feelings. Just seems, I don't know, circumstances seem to have thrown up an opportunity." Randazzo drained his coffee cup. Frankie was silent, looking at him.

"You're serious, aren't you?" Frankie said.

"Yeah, why not? We could give it, say, six months, see how it went, how we got on working together. I don't see a big downside personally, but listen, that's just me. I'm gonna go now, so you have a good think and let me know, okay? No rush."

Randazzo got up and made for the door. He opened it stopped, looked back and smiled. Frankie was sitting there stock still, looking at nothing in particular. He was still sitting there, stroking his chin well after Randazzo had left. Unable to reach any conclusion, he decided to put Sam's proposal to the back of his mind and sleep on it.

The next morning, Frankie came back from his jog, had his shower, ate breakfast, then picked up his cell and wandered out on to his lanai. Charlie followed him.

"So, what d'you think Charlie, Frankie Armstrong Private Investigator?" Then he did a poor impression of Sam Spade, and making a gun shape with his hand, pointed at Charlie. "Okay, shweetheart, drop the gun." Charlie didn't seem impressed. Frankie called Detective Randazzo. Sam answered on the fourth ring.

"Frankie. Well, what's the verdict?"

"I'm in. Where do we go from here?" Later that afternoon, Frankie found himself in Naples police headquarters, sitting opposite Chief Sullivan. The Chief was an imposing man, big in every dimension, not fat, just big. As Frankie's mother would have said, he had the map of Ireland written on his face. He really couldn't have been anything other than Irish, thought Frankie. Chief Sullivan had stood and introduced himself, shaking Frankie's hand vigorously as he did so. Frankie felt the reverberations all the way up his arm and into his shoulder bone.

"I've heard all about ye in the past, of course. Helped out Sam here on a couple of occasions." Then looking serious, he said, "although I understand it was your fault Detective Randazzo here got shot." Frankie started to protest, and the Chief let out a huge guffaw. "Had ye there, young man. Forgive me, just my twisted sense of humor." Frankie turned to look at Randazzo, who raised his eyebrows in an expression of what can you do, he's the chief!

"Now that I've given you the once over, you'll be good to go. Sam here has given my secretary all the information needed. You seem to tick all the boxes. I understand you're now a legal resident. You're ex-military and have firearms experience etc., so that shouldn't be an issue. You'll have to take an exam, a couple of hours, some nominal training, but Sam here can prep you for that. Shouldn't be a problem. My influence will speed up the process and smooth out any wrinkles, so you should receive your license in a couple of weeks, maybe less."

"On the way out, Sam here will show you to where my secretary is so you can complete the forms, provide anything she's missed or didn't know, okay? And good luck." Then Chief Sullivan stood to signal the meeting was over and once again shook Frankie's hand, and again wished him well with the new venture. Frankie thanked him for his help.

Frankie went for his training and took his exam. Nine days later, he received an email to inform him he'd passed the exam and his application to become a fully licensed Private Investigator had been approved. The following day, he received a small packet in the post containing his formal confirmation letter and his PI credentials.

After reading through the letter that came with his credentials, he sat down at the kitchen counter with a cup of tea, and reflected on the new turn his life had taken. He was excited and intimidated in equal measure. Newly resident in the USA, newly divorced, newly qualified in a new profession.... Who would have thought that at this stage of the game, my life would have such a dramatic change of direction? It doesn't seem real. He was brought out of his reverie by the buzzing of his cell... Sam.

"You must be telepathic, I was just about to call you."

"Telepathy is essential for sleuthing, didn't they tell you? Am I to assume you've received your formal approval and are now a fully licensed PI?"

"I have and I am. So, where do we go from here? When I received the notification that I was now a legit PI, I suddenly realized, I have absolutely no idea what to do, or how we get our clients."

"Fortunately, I do. We'll do all the usual stuff, Yellow Pages, plus online these days, I guess. We'll need a website."

"I'll take care of that. We have the resources in A&B Security for that sort of thing. I'll draft something up, get the IT genius Gareth to create the site, then send it to you for your input, etc. But will that generate much business?"

"I doubt it. It's the usual chicken and egg. We need clients to recommend us, but we have no clients, so no recommendations, no reviews etc., Fortunately, we have a distinct advantage. The Naples Police department will feed us leads and recommend us for anything they feel is more appropriate for a PI rather than the cops."

"That's good news. When do you actually leave? I mean, officially?"

"End of the month, but in practical terms, I've left already."

"So, we're off and running?"

"All we need is a client."

"We also need a name, Sam. Shall we keep it simple S & F Investigations, or do you have a suggestion?"

"S&F, F&S makes no difference to me, but there is one teeny weeny fly in the ointment in that regard."

"Oh?"

"Yeah. I was going to tell you next time I saw you, but I might as well tell you now. See the guys down at Naples HQ. They like me, they'll help us all they can, shove lots of business our way, or as much as we can handle, anyway. But police humor being what it is, they've already conjured up a name for us, and it's going to stick. At least in the department. Whether it leaks out, I can't predict."

"This sounds a bit strange. I don't understand."

"Okay, well, as I told you once before, my father is, was an Italian, passed now sadly. My mother is Dutch and still going strong. My father's family were police back in Italy. My mother's family were police back in Holland. Grandfather, father, you get the picture?"

"I remember you telling me yes, but I can't imagine where this is leading."

"What I probably didn't tell you, is that my mother's family had a tradition of calling the first-born male after the grandfather? Any other boys that came along, my two brothers, got it as a middle name, but I was the first boy born into our family. Thing is, my name isn't Sam, it's Stein. Which in Dutch, and German I think, is a name often given to boys. It means stone or rock. You know, solid as a rock, that sort of thing. When it's attached to a Dutch surname, it sounds okay, as in my maternal family's name, Stein Van de Berg, combined with Randazzo, not that great, hence me preferring Sam."

"Yes, I remember the story, not about the name. But what does this have to do with our detective agency?"

"Well, the boys down at the station, they know my real name, official documents etc. but they all call me Sam, which is more practical and the name I prefer. Saves a lot of explaining, etc. But now I'm leaving to start a PI business with you, one joker, a sergeant called Adam Labors, coined a name for our agency. And like I say, it's going to stick. Cop humor, nothing I can do about it."

"I still don't understand. What do I call you now?"

"You still call me Sam."

"So, where's the problem?"

"Just have a think about our names, our first names." Frankie said nothing, trying to figure out what on earth Sam was talking about. And then the penny dropped." He started laughing until tears ran down his face. He finally regained his composure and spoke into the phone.

"Frank and Stein."

"You got it," said Sam.

CHAPTER 7

PRESENT

The morning after their gruesome discovery of Billy Fairman's body, Frankie felt tight, stressed and in need of exercise. After a slow gentle jog around Venetian Bay with Charlie, he drove to the beach and went for a run along the shore. At the end of his run, he walked into the waves, then dived in for a refreshing swim.

Invigorated and energized, Frankie dried off and drove to The Big Hit boxing gym in the Naples Mall where he did half an hour on the weights, then another half hour on the punchbag. Back home, he showered and breakfasted and felt relaxed and ready for the day. Sitting at his PC, he downloaded the picture of the note and the video of the crime scene and emailed them over to Sam, then went to make some tea and to give Randazzo a few minutes to look at the picture and video.

He was sipping his tea when Sam called him back.

"Hi Frankie, took a look at the stuff you just sent over. It doesn't tell us any more than we knew already. No indication of a real struggle, just the clothes rack pushed over. I think it was pushed over to give an impression of a fight. I've seen enough crime scenes to recognize a genuine one from a setup. And to make that sort of entry wound, the shooter had to be standing next to the victim. Ergo, Billy knew the shooter well to let them get that close without being suspicious."

"So, where do we go from here?"

"I called Ross Sharkey earlier, and she emailed me all the stuff she had on Billy Fairman, which isn't a lot. He comes from Memphis. On his job application, he gave his mother's name, a Mrs. Louise Fairman, as the next of kin, along with an address. The agency who put him forward as a candidate, All Stars, there's original for you, they have no more than that either."

"No Social Security number?" asked Frankie.

"Apparently not. Billy kept saying he'd produce it, but never did. Ross Sharkey says she wasn't sure about him at all, but says the resemblance to Ricky was so remarkable, they overlooked the normal protocols. He'd only worked for them for five or six weeks. She has no more than that. No phone number contact for the mother and the phone company can't provide one either."

Do you know if your replacement detective guy, Dale whatsisname, had been in touch with Ross?"

"No, I asked, but Dale ain't the sharpest knife in the box. Take him a while to assemble a plan, so, in the meantime, I need to go and talk to the mother. See what she can tell me about her son, friends, enemies, whatever. I'll see what other background information she might be able to provide. We can take it from there. I booked a flight from Fort Myers to Memphis leaving in a couple of hours, so I'd better get going. You okay to stay and carry on with the security detail?"

"I am."

"Sharkey says he thinks they're going to start shooting some Everglades sunset scenes later today, so maybe call Clive Suman and make arrangements to meet up.

"Try to get close to Jordan, see what you can find out about where he came from, as much history as you can. Relationships, single, married, or divorced, etc. Or maybe he's gay? Whatever. You know the drill."

"Okay Sam, no problem, will do. Have a safe flight and call me if you find out anything interesting, or even if not. Speak later."

"Sure thing Frankie. Oh, make sure to take some mosquito repellent stuff to the shoot. Those little critters love dining out in the evenings, they'll bite you to death out there."

Frankie called Susman and arranged to meet them at the Eagle Creek Shopping center on the 41 at 4:00 p.m. From there, it was a short drive into the Everglades. Frankie checked his Smith & Wesson 9mm, then slid it into the holster.

He pulled on a yellow T-shirt, then a long sleeve light blue overshirt to cover the presence of his gun and enable him to roll down the sleeves should the mosquitoes decide to feast on his arms. Attire complete, he looked at his watch and left for the short journey to south Naples and the movie shoot.

CHAPTER 8

THE CONVERSATION

"Hello Sir. We haven't spoken in quite some time. You need something?"

"You recognized my number?"

"Of course, yes."

"You have me in your contacts list?" the voice said with more than a hint of incredulity?

"No sir, of course not. I just have an excellent memory for numbers."

"Okay. May I speak freely?

"We're on a secure line, so yes."

"I want you to do me a favor, well return the favor, I guess. This one's strictly off the books, and needless to say, extremely confidential, understood?"

"Understood, sir, and it will be my pleasure. What would you like me to do?"

"There's a private dick sniffing round an issue that might lead him to uncovering something I don't want uncovered. I'd like you to eliminate that risk. You okay with that?"

"I owe you sir, so... yes, I'm fine with that. Just give me the details." The man gave as much detail as he could, then said,

"And, if you get the opportunity, before you remove him, I'd be interested in finding out what he knows, which may be not much at all. But no harm asking, is there?"

"Leave it to me sir, I have a couple of men in mind who would be ideal for this job."

"Okay, sounds good. I'll leave it in your capable hands. No need to update me. Goodbye," the man said, and cut the line.

CHAPTER 9

PRESENT

Sam arrived at Memphis International Airport, a civil-military airport located seven miles southeast of Downtown Memphis, in Shelby County. It was early evening and, although cooler than Florida, the temperature was still warm enough to be pleasant. He walked through the terminal towards the car rental desks. As he strolled along, he was quietly singing to himself... long distance information get in touch with my Marie, his favorite Chuck Berry number.

He arrived at the desk, showed them his driver's license, and collected the keys to the Ford Mustang convertible muscle car he'd ordered. When he got to the pickup area, he saw his ride was colored a bright mustard yellow. Martha would have laughed, he thought, got in and started it up. Then he spent a couple of minutes figuring out how to lower the top. Top down, he drove out of the rental lot.

It was too late to be knocking on Billy Fairman's mother's door, so he drove the short distance to Jefferson Ave and the Courtyard Marriott hotel. The hotel was located near Beale Street, with its famous Rock & Roll Museum and the Gibson guitar factory–and just a couple of miles from Graceland. Nothing wrong with combining business with a little rock and roll self-indulgent pleasure... he thought as he drove into the hotel parking lot. He took his overnight bag out of the trunk and made his way to reception. Sam wished his wife Martha was with him. He'd invited her, but she said she had too many commitments at school. Supposed to be part time, what a joke! Still, maybe we can come back for a few days sometime?

Randazzo checked in, went to his room, had a quick shower and called Martha to tell her he'd arrived safely, then made for the bistro. Flying always made him hungry. A couple of beers, followed by the hotel's Bistro Burger, did the trick. Randazzo looked at his watch. It was too early for bed, and he wasn't in the mood for watching TV in his room, so he decided to go do some sightseeing. Making his way to Beale Street, he walked along, soaking up the atmosphere.

Music was everywhere. Memphis was lively, colorful and noisy. Some people walking in front of him suddenly stopped and started an impromptu dance on the street. A young woman grabbed him by the hand and dragged him into the street and started dancing around, encouraging him to join in. Sam laughed, disengaged, and walked on.

He went into a bar and had a couple of beers, then suddenly felt tired. Checking the time, he decided to go back to his hotel and turn in. It was likely to be a busy day tomorrow, and he wasn't looking forward to talking to a grieving mother whose son had so recently been murdered.

The next morning dawned hot and muggy. Sam opened his hotel room window as far as he could, which wasn't very much. He did some warmup leg exercises as his instructor had taught him, mainly to combat the muscle damage the bullet injury had caused, then began the full range of Taekwondo exercises, slowly increasing the intensity of his moves. As he went through his strenuous routine, he wondered how he and Frankie would measure up in the fighting stakes.

After breakfast, he packed his small bag, checked out at reception, and retrieved his car from the parking lot. Setting his GPS for 5 New Lawns, Parkway Village-Oakhaven, he put the top down and drove away, following the robotic voice instructions. As Randazzo drove along, he switched the radio on and found a station playing Elvis songs. He sang along.

Some twenty minutes later, he arrived at his destination. The path to the front door was bordered by pretty flower beds. There were light blue shutters on either side of the lower windows blending in well with the pale brickwork. Sam got out of the Mustang, approached the front door, and knocked. No answer. He knocked again and heard the door chain being hooked up. The door opened.

"Who are you and what do you want? If you're selling, I'm not buying, so please go away and leave me alone."

"Mrs. Fairman?" She looked him up and down, then spoke.

"Yes, I am Mrs. Fairman. What's it to you? Who are you?"

"I need to talk to you. About your son Billy." Through the gap, he could see she was wearing a blue cotton dress with a white apron over it. He tried to see some resemblance to Billy. She had a strong, handsome face, but looked tired and sad.

"What about Billy?" she said

"May I come in please Mrs. Fairman?"

"I asked, who you are?"

"My name's Sam Randazzo and I'm a private detective."

"And what about Billy?"

"I assume the police have been to see you?" She hesitated, then said,

"Yes, the cops came this morning, told me Billy had been killed, shot to death," she said matter-of-factly, showing little emotion.

"Look it's... Mrs. Fairman, look can I come in, please? My partner and I were the ones who found Billy after he'd been shot." She looked him up and down again, then unhooked the chain, opened the door, and let him in. He closed the door behind himself and followed her down the narrow hall to a kitchen area. The kitchen was clean and tidy. There was a small kitchen table with two chairs. She sat down. Sam remained standing by the kitchen entrance.

"May I sit?" he said.

She shrugged her shoulders and reached into the pouch pocket in her apron, took out a pack of cigarettes and a green plastic lighter. She shook the pack, took out a cigarette, put it in her mouth, lit it, and sucked the smoke into her lungs. Sam sat down and waited.

"Haven't had one of these for years," she said. "Anyway, how did you get involved? A private detective." She asked in a matter-of-fact voice.

"My partner and I were taken on to work security on the Ricky Jordan movie Billy was acting in, You've heard of Ricky Jordan?" She nodded slowly, then put her cigarette out on a saucer, slowly got up, brushed past him and walked down the hallway to the front door. She opened it, turned, and nodded at Sam, indicating he should leave. Sam walked up to her.

"Look Mrs. Fairman, I know you're upset, but I need to talk to you about Billy, ask questions. You know, did he have any enemies you're aware of, anyone who might want to do him harm? Was there a woman in his life, a jealous husband, had he been running with a dangerous crowd, was he into drugs, anything like that? I need to know if I'm going to find out who killed your son and why."

"He was a sweet boy. Now please leave." Sam looked at her, shook his head and walked out of the door on to the pathway. He turned round.

"The police will probably come to see you again, ask some questions, and they'll probably ask you to formally identify your son's body."

"Why? Is there any doubt about it being my Billy?"

"Not really, the people he was working for informally identified him, so... Look, don't you want to know more? I mean, about the circumstances? Did you know what he was doing for a living, who he was working for?" She looked at Sam, still no emotion showing on her face.

"Thanks for coming to tell me you were the one who found him," she said, and closed the door.

Sam got back into his car and drove down the street, turned left into a side road, and parked. He sat there trying to make sense of his conversation with Mrs. Fairman when his cell rang. Frankie.

"Hi, I called you earlier, but no reply," said Frankie.

"Yes, sorry, I switched my cell off while I talked to Mrs. Fairman."

"How's she taking the news of her son's death?"

"Unemotionally."

"Not distressed then?"

"Hard to tell. The local cops had been to see her this morning to tell her, but something weird going on. She wouldn't answer any questions about Billy's life, or friends or threats he may have had, just didn't want to know. Look, I'm going to hang around for a while, see if anything happens. Something hinky about the way she reacted. Almost as though she wasn't interested. I know grief affects people in different ways, but even so."

"How do you mean, hang around?"

"Just keep an eye on the house for a while. She couldn't wait to get rid of me, so... I don't know. Can't do any harm. I've got time to spare, my flight back isn't until later today."

"So, you're going to sit in your car and see if she goes out? What, then follow her?"

"Yeah, but I rented a bright mustard yellow Mustang convertible, so there's a fair chance she'll spot me. But if I hang around on foot, someone's going to wonder what I'm up to. And this ain't the kind of neighborhood you'd really want to invite any curiosity. I'll play it by ear and call you with any updates."

Sam finished the call, then scrolled through his contacts list to find Ross Sharkey. He found her number and pressed call. It rang, then switched to voicemail. 'Ross Sharkey here, leave a message.' "Hi Ross, It's Sam Randazzo. Just thought I'd let you know I've been to see Billy's mother Louise Fairman, to see if she could provide any background information. Her reaction wasn't what I expected, so I'm going to hang around, see if I can find anything out another way. I'll keep you updated on any progress." Sam cut the line, turned the car round, and drove back in the direction of New Lawns Way. He parked behind a car, which afforded him a view of Mrs. Fairman's front door whilst providing some cover.

While he waited, he texted Martha. He'd called her earlier, just after he'd woken up, but forgotten to tell her what time he'd be getting back home. Providing there were no delays, he reckoned he'd be back in time for a late dinner. While he waited, he kept running the whole Billy Fairman situation through his mind, trying to fathom out if he'd missed anything. Then he ran his meeting with Mrs. Fairman through his mind looking for tells, a clue as to why she reacted in the way she did or, more to the point, failed to react.

Looking at his watch, he realized he'd been watching now for an hour and some. Apart from some pedestrian traffic on the sidewalk and the odd car driving by, there was little happening on New Lawns Way. He sighed and began to text his daughter Katya. Then, looking up, he saw a car had pulled up outside Mrs. Fairman's house. A light green Cadillac saloon. As he looked, the front door of the house opened and out stepped Mrs. Fairman.

She'd obviously smartened herself up. Her hair was now well coiffured, and she'd changed into a stylish dark green flowered summer dress. She also looked taller, no doubt due to the smart dark green pumps she was wearing. The frown was still there, the same stern, strong, handsome face. So, why the lack of curiosity about Billy's death? Why wouldn't she provide any information? Maybe she's still in shock? That could explain it, I guess. Sam watched her get into the car. As it pulled away from the curb, Sam ducked down in his seat. The car drove past him to a junction and turned left.

Randazzo waited till it was out of sight, then turned his car around, turned left at the junction and followed the Caddy, making a mental note of the license plate number. He was conscious of how difficult it would be for him to remain unobserved and silently cursed for himself for indulging in his choice of rental car. Hanging back two cars behind, he tried to keep the Caddy in view, but lost it at the next junction when it turned left again, and the lights changed against him.

He banged his fist on the steering wheel and took some deep breaths to calm himself down. Why am I getting so uptight? I have the license plate number and no reason to think anyone's doing wrong. Maybe I'm becoming paranoid? The lights changed and Randazzo turned left. It was a long straight road with a bridge a couple of miles further on, so he could see the traffic for quite a distance. There was no sign of a light green colored Cadillac. He turned right off the main highway, onto a small road, and parked. As he did so, a medium gray Honda Civic drove past on the left along the highway he'd just left. He looked at it as it continued its journey. His subconscious nagged at him. Had he seen that car before? Come on Sam, there's a million of those out there, you really are getting paranoid...

He sat for a while thinking things through, then his cell buzzed, Frankie again. He answered.

"Hi Sam, any progress? I'm out on location with Jordan and the crew, so I might get interrupted. If I do, I'll call you right back." Randazzo told Frankie about the failed attempt to follow the Cadillac. I'm gonna call in a favor and get that license plate tracked. Nora, the police detective who worked for me, now works for Lieutenant Detective Dale Vogel, the guy you met at the mall. I'm going to get her to run the plates, but ask her not to mention it to Vogel for the time being. See what that brings up."

"I meant to ask you, won't Vogel need to contact Mrs. Fairman? Won't they need her to identify the body and so on?"

"Yeah, you're right, I guess Dale will get round to it soon enough, I guess."

"Won't he be pissed off you've already been to see the mother? And aren't we obliged to keep him up to date with anything we find out?"

"Yes, to both questions. But as far as keeping them up to date with what we've found, we haven't really found anything out yet, have we? And talking of finding out stuff, you find any useful background on our client Ricky Jordan?"

"I found out he originally came from humble beginnings, but I think his parents later moved up in the world. Clive says he doesn't know much 'cos Ricky doesn't like to talk about the time before he was famous.

"What about a love interest? Anyone steady, has he been married, kids, all that sort of thing. Is he straight or gay or bi, or whatever the correct term is?"

"No one steady, apparently. Says he never married and there are no kids. Clive reckons he just plays the field. Not interested in having a close relationship, he says. I didn't ask about his gender preferences, but my guess is he's straight."

"Okay, well let me get on to Nora about this license plate and if she can give me the address of the owner. If it's not too far away, I'll go have a look see. Speak later." He killed the call.

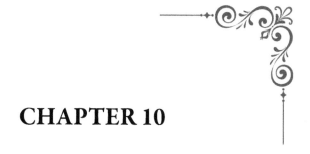

CHAPTER 10

Frankie was thinking about the conversation he'd just had with Sam. He tried to make sense of Randazzo's account of Mrs. Fairman's response to him asking questions about her son when he heard his name being called.

"Hey Frankie, can you help out over here?" The film crew were shooting a few scenes for the movie on Naples historic pier. The city had agreed to let them have exclusive use for two hours, so time was crucial. There were technicians busy organizing things. Some sound technicians with earphones checking whatever sound technicians check, a lighting guy, a couple of high-backed canvas chairs for the director and assistant to sit on, amongst a general air of organized chaos.

As part of the deal with the city, a few VIPs had been allowed access to the pier, providing they stayed well away from the action. But in their enthusiasm, some of them were now getting too close. Frankie recruited a couple of members of the crew to help him herd them away from the end of the pier and back towards the pier entrance.

The crew were now filming one of the most difficult shots of the day, which involved Ricky Jordan jumping from a fast-moving speedboat and scrambling up a rope thrown by his love interest, who was trapped at the end of the pier and in mortal danger.

The Director Clive Susman told Frankie the sequence would have been so much easier if they still had Billy as Ricky's double.

"See, he and Ricky looked so alike. We didn't have to cut and splice. We could just do the shot in real time. But now, this new temporary stunt man, come stand-in, is what we've got. He does the athletic stuff, jumping off the boat, climbing up the rope etc., which means we have to cut to a close ups of Ricky's face sweating with exertion, then back to the stand-in doing his stuff. It's all spliced in the editing room, but even so, it's a chore we didn't have before. Nobody could tell the difference between the two of them."

Frankie left Clive, to deal with a problem being caused by one very ardent fan of Ricky Jordan's. She kept trying to sneak around the tape and past Frankie to get nearer to her idol. Frankie managed to get her back and corralled her with the others. We should have strung a rope across the pier as I suggested, thought Frankie. Then someone in the VIP crowd asked Frankie if Ricky would be signing autographs later and while his attention was diverted, the young woman slid around Frankie and ran down the pier to where Ricky Jordan was discussing some matter with the Director.

Frankie ran after her but was too late to stop her from reaching Jordan. She tapped him on the back and put her hand on his arm. He turned around and his face contorted.

"What the..." he said as the girl tried to reach out to him. His arm went back briefly before it swung forwards hitting the girl hard across her face with his open hand. She yelped, rocked back, then fell over on to the wooden planks of the pier. Frankie was startled and quickly bent down to check on the girl. She was in shock, her face drained of color. He looked up at Ricky Jordan.

"I ever see you hit a woman again I'll..." he didn't finish the sentence, just shook his head. Clive Susman stood there, immobile.

"Hey man, I didn't mean to do that," muttered Ricky Jordan. "I'm really sorry, here, let me help her."

"Stay away from her and get away from me before I do something I regret..., now!" said Frankie. Jordan and Susman moved away further down towards the end of the pier. Frankie helped the shocked woman to her feet.

"I'm okay," said the girl in a faltering voice, brushing the tears from her cheeks. "It was my fault, I shouldn't have... you know... I'm okay now thanks," she said and started to walk towards the small crowd and the pier entrance.

"Can I arrange a ride to anywhere?" said Frankie

"No thanks, please just leave me alone." Frankie let go of her arm and she walked down the pier. Fortunately for Ricky Jordan, Frankie's own body had masked most of what happened. So, Ricky's crowd of adoring fans had seen very little. Frankie could see people were asking the girl what had happened, but she pushed through, ignoring their questions. He walked back down the pier, wondering what to do. Clive Susman walked towards him.

"You intending to have any more words with Ricky about what happened, or maybe more than words?"

"I was considering it, yes, why?"

"Look Frankie, these people, these film stars, as we used to call them, with few exceptions. They're always weird people. Fly off the handle for nothing, sometimes get violent. Goes with the territory. I'll make sure he pays for that incident. Ricky's got a temper, a terrible one at times. I guarantee he'll be in floods of tears about it later. It's always the same. Best leave it, put it down to experience, okay?" Frankie looked at him,

"Okay, this once. But he does anything like that again while I'm around. He won't be making movies for a while."

"I understand," said Susman and started walking back to the film crew. The rest of the day passed without incident, although Frankie and Ricky Jordan kept their distance by unspoken agreement. When Frankie got home, he took Charlie for a walk round the block, then came back and sat in front of his PC to catch up on email correspondence. He was in the middle of replying to an email from

Derek, his business partner in the UK, when his cell buzzed. He looked but didn't recognize the number.

"Is this Frankie Armstrong?" The woman's voice asked.

"It is."

"This is Martha, Sam's wife. We haven't met yet, but I've heard all about you from Sam, of course. I hope you don't mind me calling, but have you heard from Sam? He said he'd be home in time for dinner, but he hasn't showed. He'd normally call me before he boarded the flight home, but I haven't spoken to him since this morning."

"Hello Martha. Likewise, Sam told me all about you, of course, and I know he was planning for us all to get together very soon. I spoke to him late this morning, but not since. Do you have details of the flight he was supposed to catch?" Martha provided the details and Frankie scribbled them down. "Okay, I'll call the airline and then call you back. And don't worry, I'm sure there's a simple explanation." Despite his reassurances to Martha, Frankie was concerned.

Frankie called the airline and established that Sam was a no show. Then he checked all the rental companies at Memphis International Airport until he found the one that had rented the Mustang to Sam. And no, they said, he hadn't returned it and it was overdue.

"Are you able to track the car, find out where it is?"

"Yes sir, we are, but we would only do that if the car wasn't returned to us after it's been overdue for at least 24 hours." Frankie explained the situation, and the agent went to get her manager. Frankie once again explained to the manager, a Miss Percy, why he was calling. He told her he and Sam Randazzo were partners in a Detective Agency and gave her their website address so she could check if necessary. He had to wait a few minutes while she checked. Then she came back on the phone and asked him some security questions regarding Sam's identity. Seemingly satisfied with Frankie's answers, she then asked him how she could help him further, and what information he wanted. He asked her if she could provide him with the last known location of the vehicle, the GPS coordinates. There was a silence for a short while. She was obviously considering her response.

"Well, Mr. Armstrong, it's an unusual request and not the sort of information we'd normally give out, but I suppose in the circumstances." And she provided Frankie with the information. He thanked her, and she then trotted out the usual follow up annoying question,

"Is there anything else I can help you with today, Mr. Armstrong?" He kept his cool, said no thanks, and rang off.

CHAPTER 11

He felt constrained, unable to move his arms or legs or any part of his body. The feeling of claustrophobia was overwhelming. It was dark, or he couldn't see. Wriggling his body to free himself didn't work. He was still trapped, couldn't move, he was severely constrained. Oh God, I'm in a box, they've put me in a box, a coffin! He panicked. Am I underground? He stopped trying to move and listened. He could hear voices, faint, but he could hear them. He tried to calm himself.

He closed his eyes and tried to slow his heartbeat. It was thumping like a steam hammer about to explode out of his chest. His mind suddenly switched. He could see his mother now. She called his name, then he felt her warmth as she cuddled him. Suddenly, his father wrenched him from her arms and started to beat him. He fended off the blows as well as he could, then fell to the floor and curled himself into a ball. His father kicked him until his mother pulled him away.

He passed out, then woke up in an elevator ascending at speed. There were two people in the elevator with him. He didn't know who they were. The elevator stopped, and he was pushed out of the doors on to a platform. Turning back, he saw the elevator plummeting down a lighted shaft, going faster and faster. He looked for a call button at the side of the metal sliding doors. There wasn't one, no way to summon the elevator back.

He was on a platform surrounding the elevator shaft, with no more than three feet from the shaft to the edge of the platform. There were no guard rails, nothing to prevent him from falling off and nothing to hold on to. Looking down over the edge, he could see the tiny pinpricks of lights in buildings, as though from a plane. Vertigo kicked in and made him dizzy and sick. He stood with his back to the lift shaft wall, his arms wrapped backwards, trying to find purchase on the slippery metal surface.

The wind began to blow; it howled, becoming fiercer by the minute. He tried to find something to cling on to, but there was nothing. The floor was polished and slippery, the metallic wall of the shaft tower round and smooth. Then the rain came, rain so cold and sharp it felt like tiny shards piercing his body. He suddenly realized he was naked and freezing cold. A powerful gust of wind hit and blew him over and he skittered perilously close to the edge of the platform.

Sam screamed, as slowly but surely, he was pushed by the wind to the very edge. He tried to cling on, but it was no use, there was nothing to grip. He slowly and inexorably slid over the edge and screamed again as he plunged to his certain death.

Randazzo woke up in a cold sweat. He was sitting in a chair in a small bare room, lighted by a dim bulb hanging from a single electric cable attached to the ceiling. The room was empty, apart from a small table a few feet to his left with a couple of bottles of water on it. The sight of the water made him realize how thirsty he was. He took a few moments to assess his situation. His head hurt like hell, he felt nauseous and dizzy. Taking some long deep breaths, he tried to stand up but failed, gasping with pain as his arms came up against the restraints binding him to the chair. Trying to move his legs, he realized they were also bound to the legs of the chair. Taking another couple of deep breaths, he tried to stand up again, but the chair was anchored to the floor. He gave up, sank back, then realized his pants were wet where he'd pissed himself. He tried to think back.

The last thing he remembered was sitting in his car and being approached by two men. They wore masks, the kind people wear to protect themselves from the covid virus, so not that unusual these days. He remembered opening the car window to talk to them, but nothing much after that, other than fragments of a nightmare. He tried again to loosen his arms, then his legs, but it just exacerbated the pain that had increased as he'd become more conscious. He concentrated on some deep breathing in an effort to calm himself and regain his strength. Then the door opened and in walked two men. This time they wore black hoods, with holes cut out for eyes and mouths.

One man went over to the table, opened a bottle and tried to drink, but the mask was getting in the way. He lifted the mask up high enough to allow unimpeded access to his mouth and took a long glug, then pulled his mask back down. He looked at Sam, walked over with the open bottle, and held it to Sam's lips. Sam drank as much as he could before the bottle was taken away and placed back on the table. Both men now came and stood in front of Sam. They wore shirts outside their trousers. No doubt to conceal their guns. Neither of the men spoke. Sam tried to speak, but his voice just croaked. He cleared his throat.

"What the hell is going on?" he eventually managed to ask, his voice still raspy.

"Well now. Welcome back. Boy, can you scream or what?" said the man, then looked to his partner, who smiled.

"Like a banshee with a red-hot poker stuck up its ass," said the other man. They both laughed.

"Who are you, and what exactly is it you want?" said Randazzo. The man on his left turned to look at the other man, who nodded.

"You don't really want to know who we are. As the expression goes, if we told you, we'd definitely have to kill you." The other man laughed again, quietly. "It's like this," the man continued, "we've found out more or less what we wanted to know, so how about you tell us who you are and why you were following Mrs. Evelyn Fairman?"

"I thought you just said you'd found out what you wanted to know, so why are you asking me? I assume you injected me with something - sodium thiopental?" asked Randazzo.

"Boy knows his stuff," the second man said. "So, yeah, some Scopolamine to begin with," he continued, "shoulda knocked you right out, but you struggled so hard we had to sock you. Then when we got here, we gave you a little shot of the ST. Saved us all a lot of time and trouble. So, to repeat, who you are and why are you following Mrs. Evelyn Fairman?" Randazzo looked at the man and shook his head.

"Look, just indulge me," said the man. Randazzo saw no point in lying.

"My name's Sam Randazzo, I'm a PI, and my partner and I are working the security for the movie star Ricky Jordan. He's filming in Naples. His body double got shot dead and the film company management asked us to investigate his death. He's a guy called, or was a guy, called Billy Fairman, who is Mrs. Fairman's son. I went to ask her some questions about her son Billy, but she was reluctant to answer. More than reluctant. I hung around to see what she did next."

"Why? Why did you hang around?"

"Her reluctance to answer any questions. I thought there was something off about the way she acted, that's all. So, I thought I'd see what she did next."

"That's it?"

"Yeah, that's it. Look, either shoot me or untie me. My arms and legs are killing me."

"Guy's got a sense of humor," said the first man. The other man nodded, took a pair of handcuffs out of his pocket, and a knife from a sheath on his belt. Sam saw his gun briefly. Securing Sam's right arm to the chair arm with the handcuffs, the man held the knife to Sam's neck.

"Stay away from Mrs. Fairman, bud." He said, then giving Sam a hard look, poked the point of the knife into Sam's neck just enough to break the skin. Sam tensed. Then the man laughed, took the knife away and cut the plastic bonds that tied Sam's arms and legs to the chair. The man stepped back. Sam sighed at the relief, using his left hand to massage his right arm, then leaned down to rub his legs.

The lead man nodded to the other one to move over towards the door. Sam tried his best to hear what they were saying, but all he could hear was murmuring. They were arguing, one man gesticulating with his hands. Then they seemed to come to a decision. The lead man walked back to Sam.

"Okay buddy, your lucky day. We're gonna leave now," the man said, taking his gun out of its holster. "I'll put this cuff key on the floor by your feet. Try to get it before we shut the door and I'll come back and shoot you in the face, okay?" The men walked back towards the door and opened it. The one holding the gun looked back, shaking his head, holstered his gun, and they both went out, shutting the door behind them.

Randazzo used his outstretched leg to try to slide the key to within reach of his free hand. It took him three goes to stretch his leg far enough. Once done, he sat back to take a breath, then reached down to retrieve the key, but an overwhelming attack of nausea caused him to sit back up. He took some more deep breaths until it passed. He bent over again, retrieved the key, and eventually managed to unlock the cuffs.

He waited a minute. Then, holding on to the chair, stood up. He became dizzy, sat down again and breathed some more, then got up and managed to walk a few steps. The men had left the bottles of water on the table. Sam chose the half empty one, knowing the man had drunk out of that one. He looked around and saw they'd left his shoes in the corner. He sighed with relief.

He slowly walked over to the door and opened it. He couldn't see anywhere near with lights on, just a distant glow from a highway.

BACKLASH

They'd taken his watch along with his wallet and keys, so he had no idea what time it was. He knew he was in no state to try to walk anywhere, and definitely not in the dark. So, he closed the door, lay down on the bare wooden floor and slept.

CHAPTER 12

Frankie flew from Fort Myers to Atlanta and on to Memphis International, arriving at 11:30 a.m. He made his way to the car rental area and found the Alamo desk.

"I was told to ask for Sophia." Sophia arrived at the desk a few minutes later.

"I'm Frankie Armstrong. We spoke yesterday."

"We did. Nice to meet you, Mr. Armstrong. I've written down the location of the car as of yesterday. I think my manager might have already provided it to you, but I thought I's write it down just in case. But the thing is, we've already arranged for it to be collected, so it may not be there anymore."

"Okay, I see. Would it be possible to check with whoever recovered it, to ask if there was anything left in the car, any personal stuff you know, luggage, that sort of thing?"

"I can try, but it might be difficult to get hold of the recovery drivers. Any personal items left at in the car would be brought back here, along with the car. Leave me your number and I'll call you if I can get hold of them." Frankie gave her his cell number, and she gave Frankie the keys to the car he'd hired. "Take any car in row G," she said. "Good luck finding your friend." She added.

Frankie chose a blue Toyota, threw his hand luggage in the trunk, sat in the driver's seat and started the car. He took out the piece of paper Sophia had given him and set the GPS to the location. He'd spoken to Nora at Naples police headquarters, but she hadn't heard from Sam, so whatever happened, happened before he could call her. That meant he had no information on the car Sam was following, so no way to find details of the owner or their address.

An hour and a half later, he arrived at the last known location of the abandoned car. It led him to a minor road off the main highway. The road led to a gated community called Fiddlers Creek. Parked a few yards down the road was a bright yellow Mustang with another car parked behind it. Two men were standing in front of the Mustang, one on his cell and one with a clipboard, walking around the car.

Driving past both cars, Frankie turned his car around and parked behind the second car. Just to be on the safe side, he checked his gun before opening the door and stepping out.

"You from the rental company?" Frankie asked. Clipboard man answered.

"Yeah. And you are?"

"Friend and business partner of the guy who rented this car," Frankie replied, nodding toward the Mustang. "Mind if I look inside" The man hesitated. "You have a problem. Call Sophia at the airport car-rental desk," said Frankie, eager to get on. The man nodded and pressed the fob to open the car. Frankie began with the trunk and found Sam's overnight bag and his folded linen jacket. He took them out. "I'm taking these, okay?"

"Well, I'm not sure..." the clipboard man started to say, then looked at Frankie and realized Frankie was going to take them whatever the man's objections were. "I suppose, but I'll scribble a note and you have to sign you've taken stuff, okay?" Dignity restored, Frankie nodded his agreement and went to search inside the car. There was nothing else of Sam's in the car.

"Have you taken anything out of the car already?" Frankie asked.

"Just the agreement papers and this It was under the seat." The man opened the door of his car, leaned in, and held up Sam's cell phone. Frankie approached him and held out his hand.

"It's okay, I'll sign for it." The man hesitated, then reluctantly handed it over. Frankie checked it. It wanted a password. He pocketed the cell.

"Find anything else?"

"No," said the man and asked for Frankie's full name and address, then scribbled on a sheet of paper clipped to the clipboard and handed it to Frankie. He checked and signed it, handed it back, and thanked the man. Then he went back to sit in his own rental car to think. How the hell do I find out what happened to Sam?

CHAPTER 13

S am woke up. Shafts of sunlight were determinedly leaking through the grimy crud stuck to the windows and projecting strange shapes on the opposite wall. He slowly got to his knees, took a few breaths, then managed to stand up. Walking slowly over to the table, he gasped and grimaced with each step. Opening the second bottle of water, he smelled it, then took a sip, then glugged half the bottle.

He waited a few beats, then walked over to where they'd left his shoes, bent down, and with some effort, picked them up. Going over to the chair, he sat down and put them on. Shoes on, he leaned back in the chair and closed his eyes for a few moments. Taking some more deep breaths, he opened his eyes again and spoke.

"Okay, let's get to it," he said to the empty room. He heaved himself out of the chair, walked to the door of the wooden shed, and opened it. The searing sunlight blinded him momentarily. He walked through the door and let his eyes adjust to the light.

After walking a few steps, he turned and looked back at the shed he'd been kept a prisoner in. It was one of several old abandoned buildings in the farmyard. A dirt track led through to a field with a wooden five-bar gate hanging off its hinges. The ground beyond the gate rose just enough to shield his view of the horizon. Slowly, Sam made his way up the track to the crest of the small hill. He stopped and could now see a highway about a mile away. Bottle in hand, he started to make his way towards it.

Frankie jumped when his cell buzzed. Not a number he recognized.

"Hello."

"You any good at finding people?" the gravelly voice asked.

"Sam?"

"That's me."

"Sam... what in God's name happened and where the hell are you?"

"Last question first. I'll ask, hold on." Frankie could hear Sam asking.

"Okay, I'm at a place called Joe Joe's Travel Center, hang on, I forgot the rest of it." Frankie waited. Sam came back on the line, "4101 US-78."

"Hold on," said Frankie, tapping the details into his cell phone.

"Zip?"

"Yeah, MS, that's M, for mother, S, sierra 38661."

"Okay, got all that now."

"It's going to take a while for you to get here, so I'm not sure what to do. I don't really want to involve the cops if I can help it, but I've got no money, I look like a hobo..." Frankie cut him off.

"Are you hurt?"

"Nothing too serious, no. How soon could you get here, d'you reckon?"

"Probably sooner than you think. I'm parked behind an abandoned Mustang rental car near Memphis. Martha called me last night to say you hadn't come home, so I checked with the airline and the rental company and realized there was something badly wrong. I flew out here this morning and located the Mustang, courtesy of the rental company's tracking system."

"Frankie, I think you just earned your spurs."

"Thanks Sam. Give me a sec while I put the address into the GPS. Okay, looks like I'm about forty minutes away."

"Park near the gas pumps. I'll keep an eye out for you. As for what happened, let's talk about that when you get here. What are you driving?" Frankie told him, then cut the line. He turned back on to the highway, and gunning the engine, headed west.

Frankie arrived at Joe Joe's Travel Center some thirty minutes later and parked. Sam came over to him. Frankie got out and stared at his friend and business partner.

"Wow," said Frankie

"Yeah, I know. Aren't I a pretty picture?"

"Like a horse rode hard and put away wet," Frankie replied.

"I don't suppose you had the foresight to bring my luggage?" Frankie went to the back of his car, opened the trunk, and took out Sam's bag and jacket.

"Bless you. Cell?" Frankie took Sam's cell out of his pocket and handed it over. Sam grinned. "No gun, I suppose?" Frankie shook his head.

"Nope."

"Okay, just keep my phone for me until I've cleaned myself up. They've got showers here. Give me ten minutes," Randazzo said, as he picked up his bag and they walked into the building. "I'll see you in there," he said, nodding towards a small dining area. Frankie went over to sit in one of the booths to wait. He looked at the menu and suddenly realized how hungry he was. He ordered coffee and waited. Sam came back some fifteen minutes later, looking a bit more like his old self. He slid into the booth. Frankie handed him his cell phone.

"You talked to Martha?" asked Sam.

"Yes, last night," Frankie said, "she was worried sick."

"I'll bet. I'd better call her, tell her I'm okay."

"I'll give you a few minutes," said Frankie, and getting up, went over to the counter to order some more coffee, and to give Sam some privacy. He took his time and when Sam had finished his call, Frankie went back to the table and sat down.

"Martha okay?"

"She is now. Didn't tell her the details, just said I got stuck in a place with no signal."

"So, you want to tell me what happened?" The waitress came with their coffee.

"Anything else, gentlemen?" They declined. Sam waited until the waitress had left, took a big swig of his coffee, sighed, took another swig, then proceeded to recall the events as well as he could remember them. When he'd finished, Frankie shook his head.

"And you walked how far to get here?"

"Took me about half an hour, I'd guess, maybe more. A very painful walk, though. Don't think I could've walked much further. Then, like I say, the guy manning the shop took pity on me, got me a coffee, and let me use the phone."

"You remembered my number."

"Always been good at numbers, yeah. Mind, I got the last two digits mixed up the first time I dialed and scared the bejaysus out of some young woman. Must've sounded like one of those dirty old men crank calls." Sam laughed, then coughed. He took another swig of coffee.

"So, why? What's this all about, Sam? These two men, do we assume they were working for Mrs. Fairman?"

"Seems to be the obvious conclusion. But I don't know. Something weird about the whole thing."

"Something weird how?"

"Don't know, let's go ask her." Frankie stared at his partner.

"You serious?"

"Yeah, I am," said Sam, taking his cell out again. "Still have her address on here. Let's see. It looks like it's about a forty-minute drive," he said and put his cell phone back down on the table. "Let's have breakfast first. You eaten today? 'cos I can't remember when I last ate, and I'm starving."

"Me too," Frankie replied. They ordered a late breakfast of ham, eggs and pancakes, orange juice and more coffee. They were both silent as they ate.

"So," said Frankie, wiping the remains of the crumbs away from his mouth with his napkin, "if they weren't working for Mrs. Fairman, who were they working for? You said they told you to stay away from her."

"Yeah, they obviously have an interest, it's just that they didn't act like the usual low life hired goons. Pumping me full of that truth drug. I mean, these guys wanted to know what I knew, which is diddly squat. But now, I want to know who they were and why they went to the lengths they did. I had the feeling one of 'em wanted to eliminate me, but the other one persuaded him not to."

"Eliminate, as in kill you?"

"Yup that. But listen, let's not speculate. Let's go see if Mrs. Fairman can shed any light on this. I need the bathroom, then let's go," said Randazzo. Some forty-five minutes later, Sam was knocking on Mrs. Fairman's door while Frankie waited in his rental car by the curbside. The door remained shut. Sam went to look through the front windows. He came back and got in the car.

"No one home."

"What now then?"

"Let's find out who owns that Caddy, the one that picked her up." Randazzo took out his cell phone and called Norah. "You got a pen and paper, Frankie?"

Frankie passed him a small notebook he always carried and a pen. Sam's call was put through to Norah and after the usual pleasantries, Norah searched and found details of the information Sam needed. Cell held to his ear by his shoulder, he scribbled down the details Norah provided. He thanked her and finished the call.

"Here's the address and zip code," Frankie put them into the GPS system and drove off, following the GPS instruction to the address of the owner of the light green Cadillac.

478 Christina Lane was a tidy looking two-story single-family home, located on a corner, painted light gray and white and surrounded by trees. It was a neat house with a newly mown lawn and an imposing front porch.

"How do you want to handle this?" asked Frankie as they parked outside on the road.

"I think we just go knock on the door and, as usual, play it by ear. You got your piece with you?" Frankie tapped his shirt where it concealed his gun and holster. "Okay then, let's do it. I'll lead, okay?" Frankie nodded, and they walked up to the front door and knocked. Mrs. Fairman opened the door.

"You? What the hell do you want? How did you find me here?"

"I'm a detective, remember?"

"This is harassment. I'm calling the cops."

"Be my guest," Answered Randazzo. "We can ask them about your two thug friends who drugged and kidnapped me on your behalf. Should be interesting."

"I have no idea what you're talking about. And who's this person?" she said, looking at Frankie? A male voice spoke from inside the house.

"Who's at the door, honey?"

"Just some nosy PI."

"Hold on, I'm coming." A few seconds later, a man appeared. He was tall and rangy, probably mid to late sixties, with thinning blond hair. He looked at Mrs. Fairman, then at Sam and Frankie. "Okay, anyone care to explain what's going on here?" No one said anything for a beat, then Sam spoke up.

"And you are?" asked Sam.

"Not that it's any of your dammed business, but I'm Bob Harris, Mrs. Fairman's significant other, and this is my house. Now, would someone care to enlighten me?" He looked at Mrs. Fairman, then at Sam and Frankie. "You know these guys how Louise?"

"I don't know that one," she pointed at Frankie, "The other one is the one I told you about. Came to my house asking me about Billy. Said he's a PI or something."

"Okay, so why are you here now?" said the man addressing Sam. "What do you want?"

"I'm happy to explain," said Sam, "but not out here on the doorstep." Bob Harris looked at Mrs. Fairman, who raised her eyebrows in resignation and strolled back down the hall. "Show me some ID," said Harris. Sam turned to Frankie.

"You got your PI license, Frankie?" Frankie took his license out of his pocket and handed it over to Harris, along with a business card." Harris examined both. "F and S Detective Agency, Naples. You guys are a long way from home." He kept the card and gave Frankie his PI license back.

"You'd better come in." Sam and Frankie closed the front door behind them and followed Harris down the hall into a large airy well laid out kitchen. Mrs. Fairman had already taken a seat at the kitchen table. Harris gestured for Sam and Frankie to take a seat on the opposite side of the table, then sat down himself next to Louise Fairman. "Okay, explain," he said. Sam addressed Mrs. Fairman.

"I assume you know that your son Billy was employed as a stunt double for Ricky Jordan."

"I did, yes."

"Okay, and does your friend Mr. Harris here know your son was shot and killed in Naples very recently?"

"Yes, I do," replied Harris. "A tragedy," he said, looking over at Mrs. Fairman, who now had her head bowed. "So why the visit to Louise, and why did you follow her here?"

Sam told Harris how they'd been hired by the movie company, Global Films, to look after security for Ricky Jordan while they were filming down in Naples. And how they'd discovered Billy's body in the shop unit. And how subsequently, they'd been tasked by Ricky Jordan's personal manager to look into his murder on Global's behalf, and if possible, find out who'd killed Billy Fairman and why.

"Surely that's up to the cops to find all that out?" interjected Harris.

"It is, but the company filming Ricky Jordan's current movie asked us to investigate as well. Their prerogative."

"I guess it is. Okay, carry on," said the man. So, Sam told the rest of his story and about visiting Mrs. Fairman to get some useful background on Billy.

"Mrs. Fairman here acted a bit strange, in my opinion. Her reluctance to provide any information that might help us find her son's killer struck me as odd, so I stayed around and watched her house to see what would happen. Then this green Caddy came along and picked her up outside her house. Yours I assume," said Randazzo. The man nodded.

"Parked round the back. Carry on." Randazzo continued and told them about following his Caddy and subsequently being kidnapped, drugged, then eventually released after being warned off Mrs. Fairman.

"So here we are. And I want answers," said Randazzo, looking Harris straight in the eye. Harris looked at Mrs. Fairman. Her look of disinterest had been replaced by one of concern, maybe even fear, Frankie thought. He looked at Sam and saw that he'd noticed it too. Harris stroked his chin as he considered his response.

"You know anything about this kidnapping Louise?" Harris asked

"No, nothing, nothing at all, Bob," she replied.

"Well, the guys who kidnapped me seemed to be looking out for your interests. Told me to stay away from you. Why would they do that?" Sam asked, addressing Mrs. Fairman. Mrs. Fairman looked conflicted, but eventually answered.

"I don't know."

"You'll forgive me if I don't believe you, Mrs. Fairman," Sam said.

"You calling my Louise a liar?" Harris replied aggressively.

"Yeah, I am. Maybe she didn't know the details, I don't know, but I think she knows a lot more than she's willing to admit. And let me tell you something else. I'm going to get to the bottom of this and when I do, I'm coming back. You've got our contact details. If you decide you suddenly remember anything useful, then you let me know. But if I find you've been holding back, and I think you are, I'll make sure you pay, understand?" Harris stood up and slapped his hand on the table.

"Hey, you can't just come in here issuing threats. Get out of my house now!"

"We will, but one more question before we leave," said Sam, "could your son Billy and Ricky Jordan be related? Could they be brothers, cousins, anything like that?" Mrs. Fairman looked at Harris, then back at Randazzo.

"No. not possible. Billy was my only child. We don't have any relations, at least none left alive that I'm aware of." Sam stared at her for a moment, before slowly getting up from the table. Frankie followed suit. Sam stopped and turned back.

"Will you give me your cell number? In case I have any more news, or want to ask you some more questions?" She looked down at the table. "Look, Mrs. Fairman, we're just trying to find out who murdered your son. You want to help us or hinder us?"

Louise Farman looked at Harris for guidance.

"Not up to me, Louise. I wouldn't, but then Billy wasn't my son." Louise Fairman took out a small notebook from her purse, wrote something down, tore the page out, and handed it to Sam.

"Here, this is my cell number."

"Thanks," he said, and he and Frankie walked out of the kitchen, down the hall and out of the house. Harris followed and slammed the door behind them. Neither of them spoke until they were back sitting in the car. Sam said.

"Weird. She knows something for sure, but I don't think she knew about the kidnapping."

"I agree," said Frankie. "She looked shocked."

"I think I'm gonna have to call in more resources than we currently have access to. Get some background on these two."

"And how do you propose to do that?"

"Call in some favors back at the station. But enough for now, I'm feeling pretty well all in. Let's get back to Naples. I can catch up on some well-needed sleep, then take it from there. You got a return flight booked?"

"Nope, but I'll get on to reservations now and book us back to Fort Myers on the first available flight."

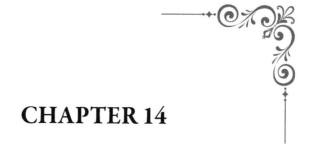

CHAPTER 14

S am recovered quickly after a good night's sleep and the following day, he and Frankie resumed their duties on the film set, having made their excuses to a very grumpy director.

"Hey Clive, you want someone to blame for us not being on the set for a couple of days? Blame Ross Sharkey, she told us to look into Billy's murder."

"Yeah, well, I don't suppose she thought it would take you both off the set for that long."

"Neither did we, but we hit a bit of a problem and Frankie had to come help me out. It won't happen again, okay?" Susman sighed.

"Okay." Then he looked at the film crew waiting for instructions, clapped his hands together and said, "Come on guys, we got a movie to make."

Today they were doing some sort of high-speed car chase in the everglades. Ricky Jordan looked as if he was really enjoying some of the fast car scenes, although he had to hand over to an ex professional racing driver for the riskier maneuvers. Despite many retakes, the day seemed to be going well.

Somehow the location had been leaked, so a number of fans who had managed to find them were determinedly trying to take their own pictures of Ricky. Frankie and Sam managed to keep them from interfering with the filming. In the end, Frankie had managed to convince Clive to agree to the fans getting a chance to briefly meet with Ricky Jordan when they'd finished the shoot, in return for them agreeing to behave themselves and keeping well away from the action. The film crew took a lunch break, which gave Frankie and Sam the opportunity to discuss their next moves regarding their investigation into Billy's death.

"Got a couple of calls earlier," said Sam, "but couldn't really break off to tell you about them. I asked Norah if she could have a dig around, you know where and when Ricky and Billy were born, all that stuff."

"Still think there's the possibility of a familial relationship between Billy and Ricky?"

"I don't know, maybe. We need to know. Were they bothers, twins, cousins or had no relationship at all with each other before Billy got to be Ricky's stunt double? Maybe it's just one of those things, looking so incredibly alike?" said Sam.

"Well, I did some checking of my own on twins and stuff," said Frankie "and found a website which claims, statistically, that every person has roughly six doppelgangers out there in the world. I find it hard to believe, but scientists allegedly wrote it up. I also found a website called twin strangers where you can upload your picture and it tries to find your doppelgangers for you."

"And did you?" asked Sam

"I'm still thinking about it." Sam laughed.

"Anyway, Norah found the information on Ricky easily enough, although no precise date of birth or location, just that he was born in 1980. Wikipedia and other websites got plenty on him and his early life. All consistent with each other." Sam took out his notebook and read from it. "Richard (Ricky) Jordan, Actor and Movie star, born in 1980. After leaving college, Richard Jordan entered The Fortune Academy Acting School in Arkansas and was spotted by a talent scout bla bla bla. In 2016, Jordan had his big break and went to Hollywood where he became the star of several hit movies etc, etc."

"And Billy?"

"No, nothing found on Billy, which is a bit odd. So, we need a way to confirm or eliminate the possibility of them being related."

"And you propose to do that how?"

"DNA would be the only certain way' I guess. The ME conducting the autopsy would have taken a sample of Billy Fairman's DNA as a matter of course. So, there's that."

"And you can get your hands on that?"

"Maybe. I'm working out how I might do it."

"And getting a DNA sample from Ricky Jordan? Without him knowing, I mean. Steal his toothbrush, his hairbrush, maybe steal a glass he's been drinking from, what?"

"That might produce a reliable sample, but no. That would present some potential logistical, legal type problems. Not impossible to do, but maybe a bit tricky if it ever got to the point of formal identification. However, lady luck may have intervened. See as part of Norah's research on Jordan, she looked to see if he had any history of criminal activity or violence, that sort of thing."

"And?"

"And he's clean as a whistle, apart from a DUI conviction about a month ago. You saw today how much he enjoys driving fast cars. Well, he was caught speeding up state. They checked for alcohol, and he was way over the limit. Convicted and fined $5,000. But the thing is, he would almost certainly have had to provide a DNA sample."

"And you reckon you can get a copy of that sample?" Sam smiled.

"Maybe. I'm working out how I might do that as well."

"What about dental records?"

"For sure, given time. And if we knew where to get the records from. And whose dental records we look for?"

"Yes, I see what you mean. Look, Clive's waving us over." Sam turned to see Clive Susman holding a girl by the arm. She was struggling to get free. Suddenly, Susman screamed and let the girl go. Frankie and Sam ran over to where he was standing.

"Bitch bit me," said Clive, looking at the teeth marks on his arm. "That hurts like hell." Frankie took a look.

"Skin's not broken, so it'll just bruise." Clive took his arm back and said, "just do your job." and stormed off in the direction of the cameramen.

CHAPTER 15

M any miles away in another state, two men named Larson and
Abner were reporting to their boss. They knew him as Mr.
Bentley but doubted that was his real name. Bentley was a big, solid
looking man with a military bearing. He oozed strength and power.
They were sitting on chairs in front of his desk, having just recounted
their abduction of Sam Randazzo and a summary of what they'd
learned.

Bentley listened intently, then got up and paced around his office.
The men watched him, trying to gauge his reaction. Bentley returned
to sit behind his desk, put his forearms on the desk blotter and nodded
his head slowly, then spoke. Bentley's face became distorted as he did.
Spittle flew from his mouth and his voice increased in volume until he
was screaming at them.

"You must be the two dumbest assholes on God's green earth."
Abner started to speak. Bentley stopped yelling, stood up, and looked
at him hard. Abner closed his mouth immediately. "You left the guy
alive? What were you thinking?" The two men looked at each other,
color drained from their faces. Bentley walked around the desk and
stood behind the men.

Then, in a low voice, Bentley added. "So, what do you think he'll
do now? Forget all about it, go back home, just put it down to
happenstance?" Then his voice volume went up by another thousand
decibels as he continued, "You... you are the two most stupid cretinous
morons I have ever had the misfortune to employ. I'd shoot you now,

on the spot, but I'm not going to. I'm going to let you live, for now. I'm going to give you the job of doing what you should have done already. Now, you go find this Randazzo guy and kill him, understand?" The last word was delivered at high volume from just a few inches from behind their heads.

The men froze, not daring to move. "I said..., do you understand? That was a question!" The men nodded in unison. "Now get the hell out of here, and the next time I see you, you'd better have finished the job. Go, now, get out of my sight!" The men got up and walked out of the door, down the corridor, and into the elevator. They remained silent until they were out of the building. Then Larson turned to Abner.

"I told you we shoulda offed him. I fuckin told you. But you wouldn't, would you? You big soft piece of stinking shit. Not sure you're cut out for this sorta work, Abner." Abner looked down at the ground. "Look at the holy mess we're in now," Larson continued, "That guy in there would kill us without a second thought. And he will, if we don't finish the job." Abner spread his arms in a gesture of acknowledgment and apology. "Come on Abner, you dumbass, we got work to do."

Frankie and Sam were early arrivals at the filming location. They were back in the Everglades, parked up in the parking lot of the Everglades Rod and Gun Club in Everglades City. Everglades City is known as the gateway to Ten Thousand Islands, but that description's a little misleading. There are, in fact, only a couple of hundred of islands in total.

Clive the Director had arranged to rent the lounge of the Rod & Gun Club for some sort of a bar fight between Ricky and the bad guys. The fight was planned to ultimately spill out on to the street, a tactic which, Clive thought, with the dramatic backdrop, would provide added 'color' to the piece.

Being early, Sam and Frankie approached the large white clapboard building, went into the club, and asked to speak with the manager. They were asked to wait. A short while later, two women approached them and introduced themselves as Patty Bowen, the owner, and her daughter, Taylor Caple. Sam and Frankie told them who they were and asked if they could have a look around prior to the crew arriving.

"Sure, just wander around as you wish."

"Fantastic piece of history you have here," said Sam. "Has it been in your family long?"

"Depends on what you call long. The original club was built in 1864, but abandoned and ready to be condemned. Fortunately, my dad saw it in 1970," said Patty, "and he could see beyond the decay and the shabbiness. He was concerned a piece of history was in danger of being lost forever and saw the potential to restore it to its original glory. So, he bought it and the rest, as they say, is history."

"Amazing," said Frankie as he looked around at the many stuffed animals and fish mounted on the dark wooden walls. A large alligator skin was stretched out on one wall. "What a great location. I guess it being featured in the movie won't do you any harm."

"It's a minor disruption, but well worth it for the free publicity. Look, we have things to do, so nice to meet you both. And like I said, feel free to wander round. I'll see you later, okay? Just holler if you need to know anything, one of us will be around." They thanked the two women and proceeded to walked around the club.

"Had any ideas about getting DNA samples for Billy and Ricky yet?" asked Frankie.

"Yeah, I think I have to ask Capt. Reagan to help."

"Won't that mean you'll have to tell him everything we've found out and all about your kidnap? And won't he be mad at you going to see Mrs. Fairman?"

"No, and yes. I was thinking of only telling him what he needs to know. Gets too complicated if I tell him everything. The proverbial can of worms, so no. I'll have to tell him about going to see Mrs. Fairman 'cos he's going to find out anyway, if he doesn't know already, but the rest, no, not for now anyway. As for getting DNA samples informally, even if we got a definitive result, it would be hard to get that to stand up in any meaningful way or in a formal setting."

"We really need the samples to be obtained legally, and formally matched, and I can't think of any other way round it than to involve Reagan and the services of the Naples police department."

"And you think he'll go for it, and maybe more importantly, share the results with us?"

"I think he will. I'll get my ear chewed off, but hey, what's new?"

"I think Clive and the crew have just arrived," said Frankie, looking out of the window.

Larson Stipp and Abner Tuffin knew everything they needed to know about Sam Randazzo. They were sitting in Larson's second floor condo in Huntsville, Alabama. They'd listened again, this time more intently to the recording they'd made of Sam's 'confession', after they'd captured him and administered the truth drug sodium thiopental. Abner made notes on a pad in his spidery handwriting. He re-read his notes, then looked at Larson.

"Okay, so we know where he lives, who his wife is, what he does for a living, who his PI partner is. We also know what job he's on at present, so it shouldn't be too hard to track him down, should it?"

"I guess not Abner. And we have the advantage, don't we? I mean, we know all about him, and he knows diddly about us. Doesn't even know what we look like," Larson laughed manically, then added, "we just have to find out where they're filming Ricky Jordan's latest movie, right?"

"Right. And that ain't going to be difficult. Pass me that laptop and let's get to it."

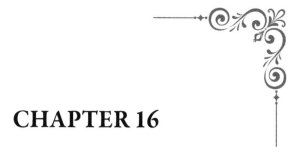

CHAPTER 16

"So, how'd the filming go today?" asked Daisy when they sat at their table outside Pepe's Pizza Parlor. The server arrived with their drinks, Merlot for Daisy, beer for Frankie. Daisy took a sip of her wine. Frankie took a big glug of his beer.

"Ahh," said Frankie licking some foam off his lips, that's better. "Thirsty work, looking after movie stars. And as to your question, good, I think, although they do seem to need to repeat a lot of stuff that looked okay to me. But what do I know?"

"And how's Sam? He getting over his recent trauma?"

"Sure is, he's back on form and good and mad about it now. And even more determined to find out what's going on. Says it's personal now."

"So, you believe the Fairman woman knew nothing about the men abducting Sam?"

"Yes, I'm inclined to, or maybe she's just a fantastic liar? But my impression was, her surprise was genuine."

"So, what are you going to do now? Got a plan?"

"My immediate plan is to finish this beer, have another one, have some wine, eat some pizza and then later, who knows?" Daisy laughed.

"Now come on, do you have a plan to find out why Sam was kidnapped, and by whom?"

"The 'whom'," said Frankie using air quotes, "is the really mysterious bit. The why was presumably, as they said, to warn Sam off investigating anything further in relation to Mrs. Fairman? But who, other than Mrs.

Fairman herself, would want to warn us off? Which leads one to believe that there is a bigger reason for finding out why we were looking at Mrs. Fairman. And some other reason for using extreme tactics to dissuade Sam from continuing to nosey around."

"What that reason is, is what we're going to find out, one way or another. Sam also reckons there was the distinct possibility they were going to kill him, but one of the guys persuaded the other one not to."

"And he thinks that why?"

"Nothing concrete. But Sam says there was some sort of disagreement just before the men left him handcuffed to the chair. His impression was, the argument was about whether or not to leave him alive. He can't swear to it, but that's what he thinks, and he's usually right in his assumptions."

"And if Mrs. Fairman has no idea who they are, how will you find out who these men were, or who they were working for?"

"I haven't a clue, but we're working on that. Maybe if we persist on looking at Mrs. Fairman, even though she may be innocent of any direct involvement in the kidnapping, maybe we can draw them out, whoever 'they' are."

"Provoke them to act, you mean?"

"Can't think of another way at the moment."

"But suppose they just decide to follow you, jump out of a car on the street and shoot you dead?"

"There is that."

"So, apart from using yourselves as bait, do you have any other brilliant ideas about where you might go from here?"

"Sort of. We've been having a closer look at Ricky Jordan. His history and background's a bit vague. We have a day off tomorrow so I'm waiting to hear from Sam about maybe going to see the Jordan's folks. Says he's got the address and contact details. Apparently, they live on a farm in Alabama. Sam's going to set up a meeting with them tomorrow."

"That sounds like a good move. But isn't it getting a bit late for doing that?"

"Sam said he wanted to leave it as late as possible to set up the meeting. Give them less of an opportunity to talk to Ricky about it. He thinks Ricky might object to us going to see them if he knew in advance."

"Yeah, I can see the logic in that." Frankie's cell buzzed.

"Sorry about this Daisy, it's Sam." He spoke to Sam for a couple of minutes, then finished the call. "Looks like we're on. First thing tomorrow morning, we fly to Atlanta."

"You know, I don't think I've ever been to Alabama."

"Me neither," said Frankie.

"You didn't say why you've got the day off."

"Clive, the Director, said something about planning the next sequence of locations and working on making some changes to the storyline and script."

"Why are you smiling?"

"Just that the script, I mean it's not exactly Shakespeare, you know. I don't know what the final product will look like, but it all seems to be predictable and corny stuff. But hey, they wouldn't produce this sort of stuff. If it wasn't to satisfy a demand, would they?"

"No, they wouldn't. Maybe people like some light relief from real life these days. Understandable, I guess. Talking of demand, I mean Ricky Jordan seems to be a big star, and his movies are hugely successful, so how rich do you think he actually is?"

"I'm not sure. I asked Clive Susman the same question. It was as much for something to say as anything else. We were having a chat in between takes and I made a remark about how much Ricky Jordan might be worth. Clive said, maybe not as much as you might think. Said he had had some substance issues in the past and was taken for a ride by a previous manager. Apparently, the manager syphoned off a lot of his money, then disappeared."

"Gee, how many times do you hear the same sort of story about celebs and sports stars? I suppose having talent doesn't necessarily indicate a coherent brain when it comes to handling money."

"Nope. Easy come, easy go, I suppose."

"You want another drink?"

"I hope this isn't a ploy to lower my defenses, is it?"

"Sole purpose of buying you another glass of wine."

"In that case, yes, please."

The next morning, Frankie and Sam were on the first flight from Fort Myers to Atlanta. When Sam had phoned the Jordans the previous day, he introduced himself as the detective looking into the violent death of Billy Fairman, Ricky's body double. He hadn't gone out of his way to indicate he wasn't a police detective. As he'd hoped, Mrs. Jordan seemed to have assumed he was part of some official investigation, and that was okay with Sam.

She also added that she had no knowledge of who Billy Fairman was, nor had she ever met him. She sounded perplexed about the whole thing. He replayed the conversation in his head.

"I'm sorry Detective, but I just can't imagine what either Gerald or I could tell you that would help your investigation." Sam countered with some official sounding mumbo jumbo about procedure and tying up loose ends and apologized in advance for any inconvenience. He put the phone down and just hoped Mrs. Jordan wouldn't contact her son to tell him about his proposed visit, at least not until he and Frankie had the chance to interview her and her husband.

The Jordans lived on a farm in Alabama west of Atlanta. It took Sam and Frankie just over two hours to drive there from the airport. Sam did the driving. When they arrived at the gates of the farm, they stopped to take stock and plan their approach.

"This looks more like a ranch than a farm," said Frankie, looking at the entrance to the blacktop driveway. It had a substantial looking five bar wooden gate, framed by some rough-hewn timber to form a traditional ranch style square archway with a wooden sign hanging from the center of the overhead piece of wood. 'Welcome to Sweet Clover Fields Farm', it said. Behind the gate and to the right, on a raised hillock, was a stone structure with the name of the farm repeated, but this time, accompanied by a professional-looking logo.

"Wow," said Randazzo, "not quite what I was expecting."

"Me neither. You could just imagine John Wayne riding up on a big white stallion and saying, 'get them horses ouda here,'" said Frankie, doing his best John Wayne impression.

"Who was that supposed to be?"

"Oh, come on... Maybe you'd like my Humphrey Bogart instead?"

"I'll pass thanks," said Sam.

"So, any plans on how we play this?" asked Frankie

"By ear as usual, I guess," replied Sam.

"Did you ever dig up any info on Mary-Jo and Gerald Jordan? Marriage record anything like that?"

"Yeah, Norah found a record of their marriage. Married in a place called Mapeletown 1981, maybe a year or so after Ricky was born? Mary-Jo Jordan (nee Anderson) was described as a housewife and her husband Gerald, an engineer."

"Well, it seems they've moved up in the world since then. Maybe Ricky did right by them and gave 'em enough money to buy this place?"

"Hmm, maybe, but would he have made enough to fund them to buy a ranch like this? I thought you said Clive told you he'd lost a lot of money?"

"That's true, but maybe he helped them out before he was swindled?"

"Maybe. We haven't really seen the place or the house yet, but indications are, it ain't no run-down old wreck. There's a phone thing by the gate. I assume we have to call to get them to let us in." Frankie got out and went to the gatepost, lifted the phone and made the call, then walked back and got in. The gate slowly opened.

They drove up the gently rising blacktop until they reached the crest of the rise and stopped. There, in front of them, some five hundred yards away, was the house, surrounded by trees, shrubs and a manicured lawn. In the distance behind the house, they could see some scattered buildings and behind those, the land stretched over another rise, blocking the rest of the horizon from view.

"I would describe that house as opulent traditional," said Frankie

"Couldn't disagree with that description. Almost poetical. Maybe you should think about becoming a realtor?"

"You saying I'm no good at being a detective?" Sam laughed. "Yeah, you're okay Frankie. How could you not be with a super sleuth to show you the ropes?"

"Yeah right," said Frankie grinning, "damned with faint praise. Well, how about you show me how it's done, Mr. Holmes? Let's go interview Mary-Jo Jordan and her husband, try to find out how they became so wealthy." Sam drove along the drive towards the house and parked.

Mary-Jo Jordan greeted them with typical southern hospitality and showed them into a well-appointed log cabin style living room. She was petite, slim, well coiffured with blond bobbed hair and dressed in jeans and a pale-yellow silk shirt. A pair of dark brown leather hand tooled cowboy boots completed the ensemble.

A large open fireplace dominated the room, bookcases on either side of it. A large red-haired dog lay asleep on the rug in front of the fireplace. An English Red Setter, Frankie thought. It raised its head briefly to assess the strangers, then sighed heavily and went back to sleep.

Sam and Frankie introduced themselves and Sam repeated the line about being detectives looking into the death of Billy Fairman. Mrs.

Jordan didn't enquire further and asked them to be seated, waving her hand towards a luxurious looking red velvet couch.

"Would you gentlemen like to have some refreshments? I can offer you freshly made lemonade, or coffee, or maybe some iced tea?" she said, looking at Frankie as she offered the tea option. They both chose lemonade. Mrs. Jordan left the room briefly, then returned and sat down opposite them. A minute or so later, a woman in a blue dress and white pinafore came into the room. She put the tray down and transferred the three glasses and a pitcher of lemonade on to the coffee table. She took the empty tray and left.

"Thank you, Annie," said Mrs. Jordan as Annie left the room and closed the door behind her. "Please help yourselves, gentlemen. Now what was it you wanted to ask me?"

"Will Mr. Jordan be joining us?" asked Frankie as he half-filled his and Sam's tumblers with lemonade. He stopped and offered to pour a third glass for Mrs. Jordan, but she shook her head.

"Not for the moment, thank you," she said. "Gerald is busy." Frankie started to pour some more lemonade into his glass.

"Some problem with one of the wells, but I'm sure he'll join us later if he's available. In the meantime, you'll have to make do with me."

Frankie stopped pouring the lemonade mid pour

"Wells?"

"Yes, an oil well."

"Oil well," said Frankie, realizing he was repeating himself like some dumb mutt. Sam jumped in.

"You said one of the oil wells, so you have more than one?"

"Oh yes, we do. Not to say that we don't farm as well, and we have livestock, but obviously it's the oil that makes the most money. So, you were saying you wanted to ask me about this man, Ricky's stunt double, was it?"

"Ah, yes, correct," said Frankie, having recovered from his amazement. He completed pouring the lemonade into his and Sam's tumblers, took a sip and carried on. "I'm not sure how much you know. It was in the news briefly but maybe not exactly the stuff of national headlines, but William Fairman, Billy Fairman as he was known, was your son Ricky's stunt double, and someone shot him to death in Naples."

"Oh dear, yes, I did know about it. Dreadful thing. My son only calls us occasionally. You know how it is with kids, they just take you for granted. Anyway, I believe Ricky mentioned it to Gerald. Told him about the poor man and some unfortunate incident. Said he and all the crew were very cut up about it about it. So, how can I help? As I said, I never met the man, so...?"

"We just wondered if we could get some background, is all. But before I ask you any questions," said Sam, "may I just say what a beautiful place you have here?"

"Thank you. We're very blessed,"

"Do you have any other children, or is Ricky an only one?"

"Sadly, we only had just the one. I probably would have had more had I known how things would turn out."

"Have you always lived here?" Sam asked.

"Oh no, we haven't always been well off. No, we were both quite poor when Gerald and I met, dirt poor, you might say. But we worked hard and had some luck and eventually got to live the American dream."

"That's good to hear. Gives us all hope, I guess. I mean, good to know these things are still possible. When you say dirt poor, Mrs. Jordan?"

"Well, I was brought up in an orphanage called Safe Harbor in Mapletown, not a particularly nice orphanage at that. And you don't start off in life much more disadvantaged, or poor. But eventually I met Gerald, and my life took a turn for the better"

"It certainly did," said Frankie. "Gerald must be really something, to have climbed the ladder, to this level, I mean."

"Oh, he is. He worked hard, we both did and we're doing okay, but like I say, I had some luck and that enabled us to get this place." Sam looked at Mary-Jo Jordan and raised his eyebrows. "Oh, well," she said, "I suppose I might as well tell you. A relative I hardly knew existed, I just had a vague memory about some relation called Jack Smithson. Anyway, he owned this farm and when he passed, it happened that I was the sole beneficiary. Somehow his lawyer managed to find me, and that's that, really."

"So, you inherited a farm with oil wells on it?" said Frankie, a hint of incredulity in his voice. Mary-Jo Jordan laughed a tinklely laugh.

"Well, yes, and no. That was the second stroke of luck," she said, "they say luck comes in three's, don't they?"

"Yeah, I've heard that. Sadly, I'm still waiting for my first stroke of luck," Sam said and laughed. Mrs. Jordan joined in. "Sorry to interrupt, you were saying."

"Yes, so my first piece of luck was meeting Gerald, my second was inheriting the farm, and the third happened shortly after we got the farm. Seems some oil company was prospecting in the area, and they found oil underneath another farm not very far from here. We had no knowledge of this, but one day this man came around, said he was working on behalf of some oil outfit and wanted our permission to conduct, now what was it, oh yes, a geological survey. He said it wouldn't cost us anything and wouldn't damage the land, they just needed to bore some little holes or something. He said if oil was found on our land, we'd be in clover."

"Right, got it. 'Sweet Clover Farm,'" said Frankie.

"Yes, Gerald's little joke. So, Gerald and I didn't hesitate and shortly after, we were told the farm had not inconsiderable reserves of oil. That's the entire story, like I say, three strokes of luck." Suddenly the door opened and in stepped a man, he looked at Sam and Frankie and didn't seem too pleased. He turned to look at his wife, a quizzical look on his face.

"Hello Gerald, these two gentlemen are here from the police. They're looking into the death of Ricky's friend, er, should I say work colleague, a Billy Fairman. Have I got that right, Detective?" Gerald was medium height, slim, had longish dark hair flecked with gray, a complexion that suggested plenty of time spent outdoors, clear blue eyes and a neat gray beard.

"Yes, ma'am," said Sam. Gerald Jordan twerked his face in an expression of extreme annoyance.

"And when was all this arranged, and why didn't I know about it?"

"Just yesterday. I tried to tell you, honey, but you were so busy with the well and stuff. Then this morning you were out of the house before I had a chance to say. Then I thought, well, I'm sure I can answer a few questions without bothering Gerald. Is there something wrong?" Gerald remained standing and seemed to be considering his response, then turning to his wife, spoke.

"No, honey, nothing wrong. I mean, you have done anything wrong." Then, turning to Frankie and Sam, he said.

"So, you're police detectives?"

"Not exactly," Sam replied. "We're private detectives and your son's manager asked us to look into the death of Ricky's stunt double, Billy Fairman, who was shot to death in Naples. This here's my partner Frankie Armstrong and I'm Sam Randazzo."

"But you told my wife you were cops?"

"No, I didn't," said Sam. "I told her we were detectives. I was a cop until recently, though. Look, I'm sorry if your wife got the wrong impression."

"I bet you are," Gerald Jordan replied.

"And what made you think we could help you with this Fairman character? I'm sure Mary-Jo here would have told you. We never met the man, nor knew he existed, until Ricky mentioned his death during a recent phone call."

"Just covering all the bases," said Sam. "you know background stuff." Even to Frankie, that sounded desperate and pathetic. Gerald Jordan walked over to the door and opened it.

"I think you two should leave now."

Sam and Frankie got up to leave. Frankie turned to Mrs. Jordan.

"Pleasure to meet you Mrs. Jordan,"

"Likewise," said Sam as they walked towards the door.

"My pleasure, detectives," she said. "Goodbye." Gerald Jordan followed them and closed the living room door behind him, then pushed in front of Sam and Frankie, opened the front door and gestured them through.

"Now don't come back and don't bother my wife again. Understood?" he said. Sam turned to face him.

"What's your problem, Mr. Jordan? We're just asking a few questions. You're acting like a man who has something to hide."

"Just vamoose, go, and don't even think of coming back." Sam turned and, taking his time, moved back so he was virtually face to face with Jordan. Then he raised his hand in a gun shape, pointed his finger at Jordan's face, dropped the hammer and slowly walked out. He looked back. Gerald Jordan was smiling as he slammed the door.

CHAPTER 17

They got into their rental and drove out of the farm, then towards the highway, Frankie at the wheel.

"You went in hard with Mr. Jordan back there, didn't you Sam?"

"I guess so, but I didn't like the man. Looks like a bully to me. You notice how scared his wife was of him?"

"Can't deny it, I had the same feeling. Bit of a control freak, maybe."

"No maybe about it." They sat in silence for a while as Frankie navigated them on to the main highway.

"So, any thoughts about what we learned today Sam?"

"Yeah, I do, just trying to separate rational thought from emotional ones. I got a real funny feeling about that guy."

"In what way?"

"He was sorta scared. At least he was when he heard my name."

"You mean you think he's connected to your kidnapping guys?"

"Possible. But maybe I'm misreading the signals. Then again, maybe we just poked a hornet's nest? What do you think of Mary-Jo's story about her unusual run of luck? I mean three pieces of luck... my ass!" Frankie laughed.

"Yeah, hilarious. Took me all my time to keep a straight face."

"Me too. When she talked to us about her three strokes of good luck, I felt I was back on my grandma's knee being read fairy stories."

"Cynic," said Frankie laughing again."

"And some. What's the chances of inheriting a farm from a previously unknown wealthy relative, then finding liquid gold on it! I mean come on.... A perfect example of the golden rule of sleuthing.?"

"Always be suspicious of coincidences?"

"Correct. And bullshit stories. And I'm still unhappy about why we can't find Ricky Jordan's birth record, nor Billy Fairman's. I'm not happy about that at all."

"Could someone have erased the records, d'you think?"

"It's possible. If there's been some jiggery pokery and the people involved have enough money, they'll make any potential problems disappear."

It was a clear sunny day, and traffic was light. They drove along in silence for a while, each lost in their own thoughts.

"You know, there was something else a bit strange. I mean, about how guy Gerald acted when we left."

"How so?"

"Dunno Frankie. When I shot him with my hand, he sort of smiled. I can't quite figure it, but it was the wrong reaction. Like he knew something. Call me paranoid, but I think we need to be very vigilant and alert for a while."

"Knew something like what?"

"Haven't a clue, but we should think about being extra vigilant and careful until things shake out a bit more."

"Okay, whatever you say, Sam. On another matter, did you make any progress in getting Ricky and Billy's DNA? I mean, if they match, that would be something, wouldn't it?"

"No progress so far. I'm still waiting for a call back. But even if they were a match, where does it get us? Not saying it wouldn't be a significant factor, but not really a clincher. It might prove they were related, or brothers even, or maybe not related at all. But even if it did prove they were related, it doesn't mean Ricky Jordan killed Billy Fairman, does it? He may not have known Billy was his brother, for instance, or vice versa. Unlikely, it was that way though, Billy being the one who applied for a job with Ricky and not the other way round."

"Course, someone else might have known they were brothers and didn't want Ricky or anyone else finding out. Wouldn't that be another possible motive behind the shooting?"

"Yeah, you're right. It's complicated, a riddle wrapped in a mystery. We need some hard facts."

The same day Frankie and Sam had traveled to Alabama, Larson Stipp and Abner Tuffin had driven overnight from Huntsville to Naples. It took them over ten hours, but Larson considered taking a car a necessity so they could discretely carry the long-range rifle and other weapons they needed. They also had to have the means to ensure a speedy getaway once their mission was completed. They'd successfully discovered the general area where Global Films were shooting Ricky Jordan's latest movie, and after a nap in the car near Naples, they went to find the precise location.

Filming had moved back to the Everglades for a few days. Stipp and Tuffin finally located the action and hung around all day with the other fans, Larson being driven to distraction by the mosquitos. They couldn't see anyone who looked like Randazzo. The film crew seemed to be handling the security themselves and doing the work of keeping the fans back.

Nevertheless, Larson and Abner both became fascinated with the process of filming the various scenes, although Abner found it confusing.

"When that guy shot the other guy just now, he took far too long to go down. I mean, in real life, he woulda dropped as soon as the bullet hit," he said to Larson, shaking his head.

"You dumb jerk. They tidy all that shit up in the editing room. When you see it on the screen, it'll look real enough." Abner remained silent, stung at being called dumb. After a few minutes, he spoke again.

"You think maybe that Randazzo guy's not working security on this gig any more Larson? Maybe the info we got wasn't good?"

"Yeah, maybe, but the boss don't get much wrong, Look, let's call it a day, come back tomorrow. These blood suckin' bugs are driving me insane. I need some repellent or somthin'. They don't seem to like you, but me, they can't get enough of. If Randazzo's not here tomorrow, not sure what we do. No good going to his home. We pop him in his own place, cops would smell a rat. Best if we can do him out here. Yeah, out here would be best. Maybe they'll think it's a hunter's stray bullet, accident, whatever. Who cares?"

"So, you plan on killin' him with the rifle then?"

"Best way. Shouldn't be too difficult. Plenty of cover. And if we're lucky, there might be some more scenes where they're shooting guns. Be too late by the time they realize some live rounds were flying around. And lots of folks hanging here. All those dumb fans. Be great to see them scatter when they realize what's happening. Great cover for a getaway as well. I hope you remembered to put them false plates in the trunk Abner?"

"Sure did boss."

"Good, now let's skedaddle, get me some stuff for these bites and find somewhere to get a big old steak, I'm famished

CHAPTER 18

The phone on his desk rang. Mr. Bentley answered.
"Hello."

"It's me," said the caller.

"Yes, I know who it is. Why are you calling?"

"Okay to speak openly?"

"This line's encrypted, so go ahead."

"That detective. He has another guy with him now, his partner.
Guy called Armstrong, Frankie Armstrong." Bentley didn't reply
immediately. "You still there?"

"Still here. Frankie Armstrong, you say. Okay, we'll include him in
the plan. I'll update my men and have him dealt with as well. Look, sit
tight. My operatives have will eliminate the threat, permanently, so just
keep cool, okay?"

"These the same two bozos who left the Randazzo guy alive last
time?"

"They are, but this time there's no misunderstanding. And they
have a very strong incentive to finish this. They don't kill him, and now
his partner too, they pay with their own lives. Don't worry, it will all go
away soon?"

"Okay, but if the big man finds out..."

"He won't. No need to bother him with this. I said, we're taking
take care of it."

"Yeah sorry, sure, sure thing, er, understood."

"Good," said Bentley, and cut the line. His next call was to Larson Stipp.

"Am I glad to see you guys back," said Clive Susman when Frankie and Sam arrived back on the set. "We messed up, Lord knows how many takes yesterday in between trying to control the fans. You made any progress on finding Billy's killer?"

"Some maybe," said Frankie, "but it's work in progress, you could say. Where's Ricky, can't see him anywhere?"

"Took the morning off. We don't need him until after lunch, so he's having the morning with some chick he met. We're shooting some stuff about the guys who are plotting to hunt him down, so not necessary for him to be here till later. Say, you two know about guns, don't you?"

"Yeah, why?" asked Frankie.

"There's going to be some more gun action today. The guys looking for Ricky have a big fall out and one guy shoots the other. I want you to check out the weapons again and make sure everything's okay. Make sure we're using blanks. I know I'm stating the obvious and I know you checked them out a couple of days ago, but I don't like taking chances. We can't be too cautious in my book. Now please keep those fans away from the set."

"Sure thing," said Sam.

"Frankie, you go check the guns and ammo and I'll go see how many fans we got to deal with today. Okay."

"Got it," Sam. And Frankie went off to ask Clive where the guns were.

The morning's filming went to schedule for a change, and at 1:00 p.m. everyone took a break while Clive Susman prepared for the first scene of the afternoon. Ricky Jordan had turned up, ready for the next sequence. This scene involved Ricky Jordan being chased through the everglades with the girl he'd rescued from her kidnappers. The kidnappers in hot pursuit and shooting at the couple, who dodge the bullets. Occasionally, the chasers stopped so Jordan could return fire. Part of the sequence was aerial shots being filmed from a helicopter. This also involved chasing Jordan and the girl, interspersed with the shots of the action on the ground.

Clive Sussman explained to Sam and Frankie during a coffee break, that the end product would appear as though much ground was covered by the fleeing couple, but it would in fact all be filmed in the immediate area and manipulated later to produce the require effect.

Frankie and Sam had corralled the fans as far away as possible, but in a place where they were still able to see most of the set. As soon as everyone was prepared, Susman checked one more time, then shouted,

"Last looks, quiet please, turn over, speed, scene one, and action!" Frankie and Sam were watching from a small clearing in the forest some distance away as the actors did their stuff, shots ringing out as the couple were chased in what was essentially a circle.

It was precisely 3:45 p.m. when another shot rang out and Sam suddenly collapsed to the ground. Momentarily shocked, Frankie looked down at his partner on the floor writhing in pain.

"What the....," he said, and was about to kneel beside Sam when a high-velocity bullet struck Frankie square in his upper back. He went down like a felled tree.

CHAPTER 19

F rankie groaned in pain but managed to turn his head so he could see Sam's inert body lying just a few feet away. There was no discernable movement.

"Sam, Sam. Talk to me Sam."

"Shut up for Christ's sake," came the muffled response. Frankie smiled despite his pain. Sam continued in a loud whisper. "If you can, slide out your sidearm without showing any movement. Do it now and be ready in case they come to check. But be careful. They shouldn't be able to see us lying in this grass, but you never know."

"You okay though," Frankie whispered back.

"Wouldn't go that far, couple of broken ribs, at least I'd guess. Hurts like the devil. You?"

"Can't tell, other than I feel like someone took a sledgehammer to my back. I just hope there's no permanent spine damage."

"Least we're still alive. Look, just play possum till we're sure they've gone, okay? If they do come and find we're not dead, it'll be a head shot to finish us off, so don't hesitate, shoot to kill the bastards."

"Be my pleasure," Frankie replied and closing his eyes, he concentrated on listening for any telltale sounds of someone approaching.

A few minutes later, Frankie heard the rustle of leaves as someone made their way slowly through the undergrowth. The rustling sounds increased. Now, there was a sound of leaves being swished as the person walked through the bushes, closer and closer. One person, Frankie reckoned. He was sure Sam had also heard the noise. Question is when to turn and shoot? The swishing became louder now.

Frankie judged his moment and turned over, simultaneously moving his gun from his side to point in the direction of the last swish he'd heard–his finger on the trigger, beginning to pull. He was momentarily distracted by seeing Sam making a similar move in his peripheral vision, but as he finally pulled the trigger, he just managed to narrowly miss shooting Jimmy, one of the production runners. Jimmy screamed and held his hands up.

"Holy shit Jimmy, I nearly killed you!" said Frankie. Jimmy's face was completely drained of color. He lowered his hands, opened his mouth as if to speak, but seemed unable to. Sam started to laugh, his laughing interspersed with cries of agony. Jimmy finally found his voice.

"What the hell!" he said, "Clive sent me to look for you."

"Get down on the floor Jimmy, we may have an active shooter," said Sam. Jimmy just stood there looking at Sam.

"A what?" said Jimmy, clearly confused. Just then, a shot rang out. Jimmy dived to the floor. Sam began laughing again.

"What's so funny?" said Jimmy, crouching on his knees.

"I think that's one of the actors shooting a blank," said Sam once he'd managed to stop laughing.

"You think the shooter is still here?" asked Frankie?

"Probably not. Been too long now. I reckon he, or they, already fled. Soon find out," said Sam. "Here Jimmy, help us both up, will ya?"

"Sure thing."

Both Frankie and Sam stood up with some difficulty. Jimmy helped them off with the Kevlar vests they were wearing under their shirts.

"You okay, or do you need to see a doctor?" asked Sam.

"No, I'll live," said Frankie, "but it's going to be a bitch later. I might need something strong for the pain. But what about you?"

"Same," said Sam, rubbing his chest. "Nothing you can do about broken ribs. Been here before. Just gonna be a matter of time. Better than being dead, though."

"Amen to that," said Frankie.

"Do I need to bring Clive over?" asked Jimmy.

"No, not necessary." Then Frankie listened while Sam told Jimmy a story that was far from the truth but provided cover for what had just happened. Sam explained that they'd been warned about a former criminal that Sam had put away, but who had recently been let out of jail. Sources within the prison had told the authorities of threats the criminal had voiced whilst coming to the end of his sentence.

These mainly focused on getting even with the scumbag detective who'd put him away, etc. Sam explained that they'd decided to take precautions and it turned out to be a wise decision. Jimmy showed concern, but mainly, it seemed, for the safety of himself.

"I'd better get back and tell Clive. He'll be wondering where I am." He started to make his way back, then stopped and turned round. "Supposing the guy comes back to finish the job?" Sam explained that was highly unlikely, for a number of reasons. Now the man had attempted to kill them, he explained, the would-be assassin would, without doubt, wish to put as many miles as possible, between him and his intended victims. Plus, he would know the authorities would be looking for him to question him about the incident etc. etc. Frankie thought Jimmy wasn't totally convinced, but nevertheless, he seemed to accept Sam's story and went back to join the crew.

"So, what was all that about? Why the fairy story?" Frankie asked.

"Lots of reasons. Too complicated for a start. And we don't actually know who shot at us." Frankie raised his eyebrows. "Okay, we can make a very informed guess, I suppose. Just want to keep my powder dry. Jimmy's going to tell Clive and no doubt the rest of the crew what's just happened, including Ricky Jordan. Who, don't forget, is the stepson of the guy who just might have had a hand in setting this up. Although maybe it's not him at all. Maybe he's involved, maybe not, I don't know. But this has all got to be connected to Mrs. Fairman and my kidnapping somehow."

"We've got to get to the bottom of this and find out why the hell someone wants to kill me. Now you as well, it seems."

"Agreed," said Frankie, "so what next?"

"Well, first, I'm going to talk to Captain Reagan. Tell him what just happened, ask for access to the traffic cameras in and out of here. There's really just the one road, so chances are we can spot the likely shooters, maybe get a picture of them, who knows? And second, I'm going to find out if there's been any progress on getting and matching the DNA samples." Frankie nodded.

"Okay."

"You feel fit enough to get back to keeping those fans in order?"

"I guess so. Come on, let's get to it before I change my mind. A very long hot bath is calling me."

CHAPTER 20

Abner drove their car slowly out of the dirt track side road, where they'd hidden it earlier in the day, and back on to the road towards Naples. He increased the speed and sped away from the Everglades filming location, constantly looking in the rear mirror to check they weren't being followed. Once he was sure there was no one giving chase, he turned to Larson, raised his hand and they did a high five, both simultaneously screaming a loud yahoo noise in celebration.

Abner turned his attention back to the road and banged the steering wheel a few times with his hands in a further demonstration of joy.

"Man, did we drop those two bozos? Like shootin' fish in a barrel. Went down like two sacks of shit. Man, that was good."

"Shoulda gone back to check really, but don't see how they could be anything but stone-cold dead." Larson replied. "I don't miss at that sorta range." The car was speeding up now as Abner floored the accelerator. "Whoa buddy, slow down there. Don't want to get picked up by no traffic cop, now do we?"

"Yeah, sorry Lars, just a bit excited. You gonna call the man?"

"Let's celebrate with a few beers first Abner. I'm too wired to talk to anyone just now. Anyways, I need a shower first, get all this bug repellent shit off me. Then let's find us a bar and maybe some company?"

"Sounds good to me, but you don't think we should tell the man, mission accomplished first?"

"Yeah, I guess so," Larson pulled out his cell, and punched in the number. The phone was answered on the second ring. "Mr. Bentley sir?" said Larson, a big smile on his whiskery unshaven face. He spoke in an upbeat manner, as a man would do, wishing to report success and be complimented for it, looking over at Abner as he spoke. "Sir, mission accomplished sir." Abner looked from the road to Larson, smiling and nodding. Then Abner heard a loud, angry voice screaming down the phone at Larson. He frowned in confusion as his partner's face crumpled.

"I, I don't understand. We saw them drop, bullets hit 'em both square. One in the chest, the other one center of his back. No way I coulda missed, and no way they coulda survived."

"No siree, I'm not calling you a liar, Mr. Bentley. Yes, I have heard of Kevlar vests...Oh shit, you mean they was expecting us? But how can you know so soon they're still alive? Oh yes, I see. Yes Mr. Bentley, yes okay. Yes, we will, understood, absolutely." Larson put the phone down in his lap, wiped his sweating forehead with his hand, and dropped his head. "Sheeet! shit shit shit! Pull over Abner, now!"

Abner pulled over on to a patch of grass by the roadside. Larson got out, walked to the tree line, bent over and heaved twice, then stood upright, took a few deep breaths, then came back.

"We're in deep deep shit," said Larson as he got back in the car, "Let's go." Abner's face had lost its color and he drove back on to the road to resume the journey back to their hotel on Tollgate Boulevard.

"You got that Abner?"

"Yeah, I did. How were we to know? I mean Kevlar vests..."

"The man said it's either them two, or us two that die."

"Jesus Christ, he wouldn't."

"Are you kidding me? He'll swat us quicker than he would a fly if we mess this up again. He's madder than a wet hen." Abner was quiet for a few beats and concentrated on driving while he drove through a junction. He turned to Larson.

"So how we gonna kill 'em now Lars? They'll be on their guard for sure."

"Don't know, but I'll figure something out. I can't think straight. I need me a shower and a beer, several beers."

"You think that's wise Lars? I mean, if these guys are still alive, ain't they gonna come looking for us? Didn't you say one of 'em's an ex-cop?"

"Yeah, he is., yeah..." Lars went very quiet.

"What is it Lars, I can see you're hatchin' somethin'"

"I think you just given me an idea on how we can get them well and good next time."

"Well, come on, how?"

"Think about it. See, they don't know we got someone on the inside. They'll think, we think they're dead, like we thought they were see?" Abner squinted as he tried to follow what Larson was saying.

"Can't see that working Lars."

"Yeah, you're right. I know. Or maybe we put ourselves out there as bait. Make it easy for them to find us. Then when they come to get us, we turn the tables on them and... bang!" Abner jumped as Larson shouted the word bang.

"But how will they know where to look?"

"Haven't quite figured that out yet, but I have an idea. Let me think this through a minute.... We know they operate as private investigators, so they must have a phone number. We find out what it is, then you're gonna call 'em and squeal on me."

"I am?"

CHAPTER 21

It took Frankie all his time to get out of bed the next morning. He'd been to CVS on the way home the previous evening to buy the most powerful pain killers they had, but it didn't much help him get to sleep. Every time he tried to turn over in bed, he was overwhelmed by excruciating pain in his back. Exhaustion finally provided some relief, and he slept for an hour or so before the pain woke him up again.

He couldn't manage a shower, so settled for a body wash with a flannel and soap. His little dog Charlie, sensing something was amiss with his master, kept very close to his legs and followed him around the condo with obvious concern.

"Come on little feller, let's walk you round the parking lot, then get you some breakfast. No long walk today Charlie." After feeding Charlie, Frankie drank two large mugs of black coffee laced with Jim Beam. He called Sam.

Sam answered on the fourth ring. The first words out of his mouth were.

"When I get my hands on the SOB who shot us, they're gonna wish they'd never been born. How you doing Frankie?"

"Guess I've been worse. I'll survive. Any chance of finding out who they were?"

"Just got off the phone to the Cap and he's okay with us checking out the camera footage. That's the good news."

"Oh?"

"Yeah, the bad is the DNA samples don't match."

"That sucks."

"It do buddy. Might have provided a very convenient and likely motive for something or other, a clue even. Still, something very hinky about this whole thing. Guy gets shot dead, we start looking at the mother and I'm kidnapped, beaten up, given a truth drug to find out what I know. These scumbags aren't your average dumbass hoodlums. Something a bit more... I don't know, the sorta thing pros do. Then the attempted assassination yesterday."

"So, they thought we knew more than we did..., or do," said Frankie. "We didn't, but they're still coming after us? That must mean they think we're going to find something out. Something so dangerous for someone, they're willing to kill us to stop us from discovering more."

"Sounds like a very likely scenario."

"So, when can we look at the camera tapes?"

"I'll pick you up in half an hour, okay?"

"What about the film set?"

"I've asked an old buddy and ex-cop Randy Keys if he and his buddy Dan would cover for a few days, and they will. It'll cost us, but we got to find out what the hell is going on. They're gonna try again when they find out they failed, and next time they'll make sure."

"Randy Keys?" said Frankie.

"Yeah, I know. And yes, it's his real name," Sam replied.

"So, you reckon they'll try again?" said Frankie.

"I'm positive. We've walked into something bad here." Sam picked him up and they drove to police headquarters. They were escorted to an office with blanked out windows and introduced to the man in charge, Gus Walters. They sat with Gus in a room with multiple screens switching views of various parts of Naples and the surrounding roads. Gus asked questions and made notes on the location of the attempted assassination and the likely times of the car departing from the scene.

103

"You're sure these guys would be fleeing the scene in a vehicle and not on foot?" asked Gus

"Can't say a hundred percent, but it's very unlikely they would try to flee through the Everglades on foot, just too many obstacles, canals, swamp, plus snakes and gators. No, I'd put money on them driving away. And as there's only one road in and out of there, they went one of two ways, east or west."

"Okey dokey, now let's see." Gus played the keyboard in tandem with the mouse and pretty soon they were looking at all vehicles traveling along the 41 otherwise known as the Tamiami Trail, during a forty-minute time slot. That being twenty minutes on either side of the time, Frankie and Sam were shot. They decided to look at vehicles traveling west towards Naples first.

Sam felt it unlikely the assassins would have traveled all the way from Miami on the eastern coast. Naples was fifteen to twenty minutes away, whereas Miami was well over an hour's driving time. Using the automated license plate system, Gus could quickly to show them who owned any vehicle passing past the camera. Traffic was fairly light, so it wasn't too difficult to pick out any likely vehicles for further inspection. A white GMC Sierra drove past.

"Stop there Gus and rewind please," said Sam. Gus did as he was asked and rewound until they could see the driver more clearly. It was an older woman in a Stetson hat with a big gray dog sat on the passenger seat. Gus looked at Sam, who tilted his head and smiled, "Nope, don't think so, carry on."

There was a long break in the traffic, then a gray Chevrolet Silverado pickup truck hove into view and went past the camera. Frankie said "Stop, can you rewind a bit again Gus?" Gus obliged. "Nope, another woman driving. Unlikely." They went through a similar process for another five vehicles, then a dirty beige Ford F series pickup passed by. "Wind back Gus. Two men in that truck, I'm sure." Gus wound the film back and froze the frame it at the point of the best view of the two men.

"Are they high fiving?" asked Frankie. Sam replied.

"From the expression on their faces, I'd say they seem very happy about something. Run it on a tad Gus please. "Yup, high fiving. Check the plate, will you Gus?"

"Already on it," said Gus. "Hmm... the plate and the make of vehicle don't match."

"I think we maybe got us our assassin boys," said Sam.

"You want me to check the other cameras further up that road? I can do that, but it's gonna take some time. So why don't you boys go get a coffee or something? With all due respect etc., I concentrate better without you looking over my shoulder."

"Understood Gus," said Frankie, "back in half an hour?"

"Make it an hour, okay? I got some other things I got to do as well."

Frank and Sam went out of the police headquarters and drove into Naples to find a coffee shop. They parked on 13th and walked to Jane's Cafe on Third Street and sat at an outside table, both wincing as they sat down.

"Still sore?" said Frankie.

"Yeah, like you're not? You sat down like an old man on his last legs." Frankie laughed.

"I'll soon repair, had worse. Just can't wait to get my hands on those two mouth breathers"

"Yeah, but what I'm really looking to is finding out who's running the show, who's behind this, and what it's all about."

"You bring Captain Reagan up to date?"

"I did, mostly anyway. He's warned me not to jump to conclusions."

"Oh?"

"Yeah, I told him about the camera tapes. The timing, the guy's high fiving and the phony number plates. He agrees they seem a good fit, but as he said, we have nothing concrete to prove these are our guys.

Says if we take this forward, it's on us. He can't take any action without some solid basis, enough proof to arrest these men. Assuming we can find them."

"What about ballistics? Matching any of those bullets to their rifle, assuming they have one with them."

"In my experience, it's not that easy unless you have an undamaged bullet, which I very much doubt they'd find at the scene. Or brass casings, which we don't have either, so..."

"You have any doubt it's them, though?"

"Got to be some doubt, yeah, but my gut says it's them. And whoever it is they're working for has a wide sphere of influence. I wonder if our client, the mega star Ricky Jordan, knows what's going on. Probably nothing, but our visit to both Billy's mother and his folks triggered a violent response. And his father's behavior when we left..., something not right."

"Maybe go talk to Ricky's father again later."

"Yeah, maybe, but first let's see what we can find out about our would-be assassins. I think they remain a clear and present threat to us, Frankie boy." Sam looked at his watch. "Come on, finish your coffee and let's go back."

Gus had managed to track the vehicle all the way up the 41 into South Naples, then north along Collier Boulevard. Frankie and Sam looked intently at the screens as Gus showed them the journey tracked by traffic and red light cameras.

"Now this is where we lose the vehicle. We have it south of the junction of Collier and Beck Boulevard, but I couldn't see anything north of that junction, so they didn't turn on to Interstate I-75. I can't pick them up going west or east on Beck Boulevard, so chances are they turned off around here," Gus said pointing at an area he'd zoomed in on, on Google Earth, which he'd brought up on an adjacent screen.

"Tollgate Boulevard." said Frankie. "Hmm, three hotels in that immediate area," he said, and pointing at one, then the other, reeled off the names. "Holiday Inn Express, Comfort Inn and Super Eight." Sam had taken his notebook and pen out of his jacket pocket and noted them all down. "You can see why they chose this area. It's right next to the slip roads leading on to the I -75. They can choose to go east or west. But they haven't done yet, so logic says they've gone back to one of these hotels. They would need a local base if they're out of towners, and I'd bet my life they are."

"Makes sense," Sam replied. "Now, if these are the guys we want, and they think they've completed their mission successfully, i.e... offing us two, then what do they do? Do they stay and celebrate, or hightail it back to where they came from?"

"Good question Sam." Frankie looked at his watch, "Look, I need to get back to my condo, take Charlie for a walk. Maggie, she's the neighbor who usually walks him if I'm not there. She's gone to visit her son. Sorry about this."

"No, listen, if you don't mind, I'll come with you, and after you've walked Charlie, we can sit down over a coffee and make some sort of plan.

Charlie was delighted to see Sam, and did a little dance of joy around his legs when they entered the Condo, only stopping when Sam bent down and ruffled his hair.

"Hello little feller," said Sam. Duly acknowledged Charlie, then went to Frankie and sat at his feet, looking up at him in a meaningful way.

"This dog might as well be speaking. That look says I'm overdue a walk," said Frankie, who laughed and took Charlie's leash from behind the door. "Help yourself to coffee or anything else, back in fifteen minutes." Sam made some coffee, walked out on to the lanai and gazed out over Venetian Bay.

"What a great view to wake up to," he said out loud and sighed a weary sigh. He sat on one of the lanai chairs, his face creasing with pain as he did so. Once he was reasonably comfortable, he sipped his coffee, then put the cup down on the lanai table and nodded off. He was woken by the simultaneous sounds of door the condo opening and his cell phone buzzing. Standing up gingerly, he took his cell out of his trouser pocket with this right hand and waved at Frankie with the other. He pressed the button and answered the call.

"Is that F and S Investigations?" They didn't get many cold calls. The only leads so far were referrals from his old police colleagues, so he was always forewarned. Sam was confused for a moment.

"It is. How'd you get this number?"

"It's on your website, dummy." Sam was a bit taken aback at the insult but ignored it.

"Yes, of course it is. What can I do for you, er Mr....?"

"Your partner there with you?" Sam looked around at Frankie and used his finger to summon Frankie over to the lanai. Frankie hung Charlie's leash up behind the door and walked over.

"Why do you wanna know?" said Sam

"Put me on speaker," came the reply. Frankie was now at Sam's side mouthing, who is it? Sam raised his eyebrows and shrugged his shoulders, then he pressed the speaker button.

"Okay, you're on speaker and my partner's here now. Who are you?"

"I'm the guy who was with the guy who shot you." Sam looked at Frankie, his face in a frown.

"How' d'you know you didn't kill us, how d'you know we were still alive?" There was silence at the other end. The caller obviously hadn't thought that through, Sam concluded. The man continued.

"Listen, it wasn't my idea, killing you an all. I didn't sign up for no murder job. I want out. But my buddy, he's crazy."

"Okay," said Frankie, "so what is it you want? I assume you didn't call just to apologize."

"I wanna do a deal. If I lead you to my buddy, the crazy guy, can you promise me I'll be off the hook? I won't go down with him?" Sam looked at Frankie and pointed at himself. Sam answered.

"So, you give him to us and then you walk. That's the deal?"

"That's the deal," came the reply.

"So, we just give you our word you'll get off the hook and you tell us where the shooter is, right? You're a very trusting guy."

"Yeah well. Look, you want the deal or not?" The man sounded on edge.

"Yeah, we want the deal," said Sam, "Where is he and what's his name?"

"Not so fast. He's holed up. We'd planned on going back tomorrow, so it'll have to be tonight. I'll meet you and take you there. Just you two, no cops understand? If I even think there're cops involved, I'll disappear, and you'll never find the guy."

"Where do we meet you and when?" Sam replied.

I'll text you in five minutes. Don't bother trying to trace the phone. It's a burner. Remember, no cops." The line went dead. Sam put his cell in his pocket and looked at Frankie.

"So, what do you take from all that?" Frankie stroked his chin.

"Quite a lot. Let's sit down and let me get a coffee. Refill?" Sam nodded yes. Frankie went and made the coffees, then came back, put them down on the coffee table and sat down. "Okay, well first off, as they know we're still alive, they must have someone on the inside, someone on the film crew."

"Or it's superstar Ricky Jordan." Sam's cell pinged. He read the message. "He's given us a place and a time. 6:30 p.m. Holiday Inn parking lot, Tollgate Boulevard Bingo." He put the cell down on the table and slid it to Frankie. Frankie read the message. "What do you think?"

"My first thought is, why on earth would these people, who just tried to kill us, think we'd fall for this... meeting the guy at this prearranged spot? We'd just be exposing ourselves to the sniper guy again... and this time, it'd be a head shot for sure. What does that say?"

"It says we're not dealing with a pair of masterminds, that's for sure. These are just a couple of guys who would normally be carrying out instructions for someone else, someone with more brainpower. Having failed in their attempt to kill us, they're trying to improvise. They're probably panicking, probably in big trouble for botching up their mission."

"So, what do we do Sam?" Sam tapped the side of his head

"We need to make them run back to base so we can follow them. I have an idea. Gimmie my cell back."

Sam phoned someone called Zak and explained what he wanted done. He gave him the time and place the anonymous caller had texted over.

"Yes, tonight," said Sam, "Comfort Inn Parking lot, Tollgate Plaza, end furthest away from the hotel. Yeah, that's the one. Six thirty. Can you do that for me? Great. I owe you, buddy." Sam smiled and pocketed his cell. "Okay, we've got the movie set security covered for the next few days with Randy and his buddy, so we need to focus on finding out who wants to kill us, and why. If I can help it, I'd prefer not to involve Capt. Reagan in this just yet."

"Who was that? On the phone, I mean."

"That was Zak, senior guy in the police communications department. He can send traffic cops racing to any destination within Collier County. I've asked him to send a couple of cars to this place tonight, sirens blaring, lights flashing, the works."

"I assume you have some sort of a plan?"

"I do. And you maybe need to get together whatever stuff you might need to take with you. If I'm right, the police cars descending on the parking lot will really spook our two friends, and my guess is they'll make a run for it. They'll be all geared up to flee the scene, anyway. Like you say, the plan is a couple of head shots from the sniper guy, then they'll be off. They're gonna jump on the I-75 and go either east or west."

"My guess is west, then north, but we can't be sure. We know their car and plate, but they might have switched the plates back to the genuine ones. Even so, shouldn't be too difficult to identify the truck. So, one of us waits on the westbound interstate and the other on the eastbound. Whoever picks 'em up, tells the other one. Whichever of us is facing the wrong way finds the first ramp to turn off and gets back on the I-75 and catches up. Then we tail them all the way back to wherever."

"Got it," said Frankie, "we leapfrog so they don't see us tailing them."

"Yeah, but not just that. It could well be a long journey, so when one of us of us needs to refuel, or use the restroom, we can do it without we risk losing them. When they stop, we just wait."

"Hang on, they know what we look like."

"Yeah, I thought of that too, so I'll buy a couple of baseball hats when I leave here, gray, unremarkable ones with long peaks. We just keep the peaks well pulled down, wear sunglasses, should be enough to stop them recognizing us." Sam looked at his watch, "We got plenty of time. I'll go back home now and put some things together, then meet you back here in an hour. We can have a think through my suggestion and make sure the plan is sound."

"How long a journey do you think it'll be?"

"Don't know. Let's plan on a very long journey, and if it's shorter, then good. Or, maybe they'll completely balls up my plan by going to Fort Myers airport and flying off somewhere?" Frankie laughed.

"There is that," said Frankie

CHAPTER 22

"You got that done Abner?"

"I did, but you think they'll be dumb enough to fall for it?"

"Maybe not, but you never know. If they don't turn up, we just lie low, for a while, think up another plan. But just in case I get to shoot the dumb bastards, we need to be ready to git, and git fast. Let's get our stuff packed and in the car. And don't forget to put the old plates back on."

"Okay Lars, you're the boss."

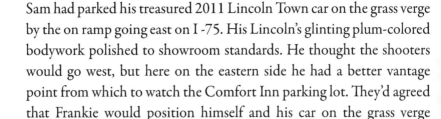

Sam had parked his treasured 2011 Lincoln Town car on the grass verge by the on ramp going east on I-75. His Lincoln's glinting plum-colored bodywork polished to showroom standards. He thought the shooters would go west, but here on the eastern side he had a better vantage point from which to watch the Comfort Inn parking lot. They'd agreed that Frankie would position himself and his car on the grass verge just off the ramp for the Interstate going west, ready to follow the car, should the shooters do as Sam hoped they would. Randazzo took out his cell phone.

"Hi Frankie, you in position?"

"Yep, you?"

"Found a nice vantage point on top of a hillock, and I'm looking down at the parking lot now."

"Anything?"

"Nothing yet," said Randazzo, sweeping the lot with his high-powered binoculars. "We got a good ten, fifteen minutes before the cops arrive and the show begins."

"What if they don't run?"

"Then I guess I'll eat my hat. Oh, and by the way, I checked in with Randy about the film set and he says everything's copacetic. In fact, he said he and his buddy are enjoying the gig."

"Good to know."

"Yeah. He also said something I found vaguely interesting. Ricky has asked a couple of times if he knows where we are and what we're doing."

"Huh, that is interesting. Although maybe it's just idle curiosity?"

"Yeah, you're probably right."

Frankie leaned against his jeep wearing his baseball cap and sunglasses, the cap's peak pulled down over his face. He caught sight of a woman driving on to the highway. The resemblance to his ex-wife Penny was remarkable, and he began to think about her. Something he had hadn't done for quite some time. Hardly ever since hooking up with his present girlfriend Daisy. She was a free-lance journalist he'd met when she interviewed him in the past about his involvement in the shark attack at the Acadiana Condo complex where he lived.

He was amazed at the combined feeling of sadness and affection as he remembered the good times he and Penny had together. That was before she decided her life wasn't truly fulfilled. Maybe she'd have felt differently if she hadn't decided not to have children? His cell buzzed.

"Highway patrol," he answered.

"Yeah, hilarious, well get this Broderick Crawford, about five minutes ago, a guy just walked into the parking lot and went to his truck. He put the hood up and started messing with the engine. Keeps looking round. Looking for us would be my guess. Could be our man. Can't see any shooter, but then I'd guess he wouldn't be exactly advertising his presence. Uh oh, here come the cops."

"Yes, I can hear them through your cell. What's the guy doing?"

"Body language says, panicking but struggling to appear casual. Kind of ignoring the cop cars flooding into the lot, which no normal person would do. The cops are out of their cars, guns drawn, scanning the parking lot. The guy's just standing there now. If it's him, he ain't going to leave until the cops do. Won't want to act suspicious. Here we go, a cop's going up to talk to him. The cop's giving him the hard stare."

"This is funny, the guy must be crapping his pants. Now the cop's walking back to his cruiser. They're all leaving,"

"What's the guy doing now?"

"He's on his cell, he's finished the call. That was quick." Sam was silent for a few beats.

"Come on Sam, what's happening?"

"Hold on... yup, here comes the other guy now. He's holding an oblong shaped bag. No prizes for guessing what's in that. He's put the bag in the back of the truck. Now they're both scanning the parking lot, no doubt making sure the cop cars have gone. Okay, now they've both got in the truck and it's moving out of the parking lot. Might come past you now unless they have to stop at wherever they were staying to collect more stuff. Keep an eye out. I'm walking back to my car now. They might come my way, but I somehow doubt it."

"Okay, I'm sitting in my car and watching the ramp in my mirror. I think this could be them now. Yep, it is! I'm letting a couple of cars get in between us. Here we go, pulling out now, and off we go."

"Don't get too close."

"It's okay, I won't. There's a truck and two cars in between us now."

"Okay, I'm committed to going east now, so it's going to take me some time to get to a junction where I can get off back on again coming west. Let me know if they do anything unexpected. I should be able to catch you up in less than an hour."

"Okay Sam. Looks like they're not going fast. Not taking any risk of being pulled over for speeding and keeping well within the speed limit."

"Good. On my way."

CHAPTER 23

Larson and Abner didn't speak for the first ten minutes of the journey back to Alabama, each wrapped in his own thoughts. Abner broke the silence.

"Didn't the man say he'd kill us both if we didn't manage to kill those two?"

"I don't think he said those precise words, but yeah, he will."

"So why are we going back to Alabama, Lars?"

"Cos, that's where we live and where our money and shit are. It's going to take us some time to get there, so we have a while to come up with a plan." Abner didn't respond for a while, then said.

"We could turn ourselves in to the authorities, maybe? Tell them about Mr. Bentley. We'd do time, but maybe we'd get to live." Larson Stipp turned and looked at Abner, snorted, then laughed an un-humorous laugh.

"I don't think you appreciate just how ruthless our employers are, do you?" Larson said, shaking his head.

"What?"

"Unless I'm very much mistaken, this operation, this mission to kill these two guys, is shady, unofficial. Maybe some big shot with a lot of influence using the Feds for his own ends? We give ourselves up to the authorities, they'd have to shut us up. We'd be better off shooting ourselves in the head now. Better than going to prison and being shanked. You understand what I'm saying?"

"You mean they'd have us killed in prison? Couldn't we ask for special protection?"

"Yeah, and they'd still have us killed," said Larson, raising his eyes to heaven. Abner was quiet while he thought about what Lars had just said.

"You sure Lars."

"I'm sure Abner trust me. Giving ourselves up is not an option, okay? We have just two options if we want to live. Option one, we kill them two detective mothers like we were supposed to. Option two is we run."

"So, do you think we can still find a way to kill those two guys? 'Cos if we were going to do that, why are we leaving?"

"I got to have time to think. I keep thinking about that show back there. All those cops turning up, sirens and flashing lights an all. I mean, what was that all about?"

"You know what it was about. The two guys told the cops we were trying to set up a hit, so the cops came looking for us."

"Yeah, but... That's not the way they'd do it. I don't know, seemed a bit..."

"A bit what Lars?"

"More like they was trying to scare us, you know, like when we go hunting, you creep up all quiet like, then make a big noise to flush the birds out so you can shoot 'em."

"But no one shot us, did they?"

"No, they didn't, but I just got this feeling, I don't know, maybe I'm getting..., what is it?"

"Paranoid?" said Abner, turning round so he could look out of the rear window, then bending forward to look in the side mirror.

"You think they'd try to tail us rather than try to catch us, or kill us?"

"I don't know Abner. I'm all screwed up. Just thinking out loud, really. Best keep an eye out, though. Either way, we got to get back to Huntsville, pick up our shit, get the cash we stowed and go find somewhere to hide away a while. Let things cool down and give me time to think about planning our next moves."

"What about Mr. Bentley, won't he know we failed to kill those guys?"

"Soon enough Abner, and that's why we need to move fast."

CHAPTER 24

It wasn't difficult to follow the beige Ford pickup along the Interstate. One thing about Florida, the weather being what it is, most vehicles were nice and clean. The dirty truck stood out like a sore thumb. As Sam had predicted, the men went west, then continued on the I-75 as it turned north. The truck stayed mostly in the right-hand lane.

Frankie stayed two or three vehicles behind. He had to be vigilant when they came to any upcoming highway exits, ready to turn off if they did. They drove along, over the bridge spanning the Caloosahatchee River, which Frankie always found impressive, and continued their journey northwards.

As he drove along, Frankie became reflective again. The sight of his wife's lookalike had reawakened something in him. He realized despite everything, he still loved Penny. She'd seemed so happy when they first married, then suddenly left him to live with a woman work colleague she'd become fond of. She told an astounded Frankie, she'd felt unfulfilled for a while and thought maybe she was living a lie by being in a heterosexual relationship.

Penny's experiment failed, and she made a tearful and remorseful plea to return to the marriage. Frankie agreed, and things were good for quite a while. If anything, better than before, thought Frankie. Then the restlessness set in again and she said she had to leave 'to find herself'. That was the last straw. Maybe what Penny was missing was having their own family? To Frankie, everything was about family. He was brought up in a Catholic household with a brother, two sisters, an Irish mother, and a father born in Yorkshire. The Irishness in him brought romanticism and humor, the Yorkshire element, practicality.

When he first visited America and Florida, he soon found empathy with traditional American values. Independence of thought, freedom of speech, the wisdom of the founding fathers and the declaration of independence–that God made all men equal and gave them the rights to life, liberty, and the pursuit of happiness.... His cell buzzed and brought him out of his reverie.

"Hi Sam, how are you doing?"

"Doing good. I'm pretty sure I can see your Jeep now, about ten vehicles ahead."

"You've made good time. You want to switch places now?"

"Yeah, why not? Slow down a little and you'll soon get overtaken. Maybe drop about five vehicles behind where you are now. I'm coming up on your left now. No waving or acknowledgement, okay, just keep the line open?" Frankie did as Sam said and was soon overtaken, gradually dropping back until his jeep was positioned nine or ten vehicles behind the truck they were following. Sam passed him and slotted into the right-hand lane, three cars behind the men's vehicle. Once they were both in position, Frankie asked.

"So, what's the plan? We follow them to wherever, or grab them before, at a rest stop maybe?"

"My original thought was to follow them all the way to their destination, which I thought could probably be somewhere in Alabama, maybe Tennessee, somewhere in that neck of the woods. But there's a serious risk we might lose them once we get off the Interstate. One, they could spot us more easily, or two, we could just lose them by accident, traffic lights, road intersections, would all have the potential to louse things up."

"The same thought struck me. If finding out who was behind your kidnapping and the attempt to kill us both, then we can do that anywhere. We just need to get them to a place where we can interrogate them properly."

"Yeah, agreed. I'm sure we can persuade these two to reveal who's giving them their orders, then maybe we'd get some answers?"

"Well, they're going to have to stop at some point to fuel up and use the restrooms and maybe eat, so do we try to take them then? We've been traveling just over an hour, so I reckon they'll stop at about the two-hour point, maybe a bit further, unless they're planning on pissing into a bottle in the car or something. So, the next hour I'd guess."

"Okay, let's do that. You bring handcuffs?"

"Two pairs."

"Good."

"Sam, talking of rest rooms, there's a rest area just coming up, if they don't stop there, I will. How about you?"

"I'm good for now. I trained my bladder well on all those stakeouts in the past. You go use the rest rooms and I'll stay on their tail unless they choose to stop as well." They soon reached the rest stop, but the men kept going, Frankie drove off the highway. Ten minutes later, he called Sam back.

"Back in position, Sam. So how do you want to play it when they stop?"

"I've been thinking on that. We're going to have to improvise. They're going to have to stop soon, fuel up, use the restrooms, maybe grab some grub. We watch them and when they leave, I'll make their truck stop somehow as they drive out of the place. I don't know quite how, but if and when I do make a move, make sure you're near so you can jump in and help. I'll deal with the driver, you focus on the passenger. They won't be expecting it, so shouldn't be a problem."

"Once we've got the situation under control, you get the guy on the passenger side out, cuff him, and get him in the back of their truck. It's a four-door, so that makes it easy enough. I'll take the driver and put him in the back of my car. You drive the truck to some place, not far away, I'll follow, okay?"

"And then,"

"We have a nice private conversation with them, find out what the hell's going on"

"Okay, got that. And if it doesn't work quite like that?"

"We innovate."

The journey continued for just over another hour before the men decided to stop. They turned off the highway and into a rest stop near Bradenton. Sam and Frankie followed, Frankie getting stuck briefly at the traffic lights at the intersection just before the gas station. He tapped the steering wheel impatiently as he waited for the lights to turn green, then drove on and into the Shell Station.

A man was already at the gas pump filling up the Ford Truck, but no sign of the second man. Sam's car was parked near the gas station exit, but no sign of Sam either. Frankie parked in a space near to Sam's car. He pulled on his baseball cap and sunglasses, got out and head down, pretended to look at his cell, whilst watching the man pumping gas out of the corner of his eye. As the man finished filling up his truck. Must have prepaid at the pump, thought Frankie. He flipped the small leather strap holding his gun in its holster. A man walked out of the gas station shop followed by another, then Sam came out next, cap pulled well down to hide his face. The first man who exited the shop approached the truck, exchanged a few words with the other man, who then walked into the gas station shop.

Sam walked towards Frankie. Frankie lifted his sunglasses briefly and made eye contact with Sam as he walked past. Sam got into his Lincoln and starting the engine, drove out through the exit, then reversed and parked on the right-hand curb side of the exit. There was no other exit from the gas station. When cars drove out of the truck stop, they had to turn right at the exit and onto the feeder road, which went around the block to an intersection which took them back to the I-75.

Frankie continued faking a call on his cell. One man had now got into the passenger seat of the Ford Truck. A few minutes later, the man who'd been filling up the truck came out of the shop, got into the driver's side and started the engine. Frankie looked over at Sam, who was sitting in his car, engine idling. Sam nodded his head once. As the truck slowly pulled away from the gas pumps and drove towards the exit, it stopped briefly and then, as it slowly turned right on to the feeder road, Sam drove his car into the truck's rear end, gently, but firmly, jolting the truck forwards. The enraged truck driver stopped and jumped out of the truck to remonstrate with the driver of the Lincoln.

Frankie did a quick check, to make sure no one was watching, then as he saw Sam start to get out of his car, moved quickly round to the passenger side of the truck, pulled the door open and pointed his gun at the passenger.

"Freeze," he said in a low growl. The man in the passenger seat put his hands up. Frankie stepped back a pace, and keeping his gun trained on the man, took a quick look over at the situation on the other side of the vehicle. Sam had already cuffed the truck driver and was pushing him into the rear of this car. The man was cursing loudly, the noise suddenly cutting out when Sam slammed the rear door. He looked over at Frankie, gave a little wave, and smiled.

Frankie turned back to the other man, scanned the area to see if anyone had noticed what was going on. Satisfied there were no spectators, he told the man to get out and put his hands behind his back. The man obeyed. Frankie snapped on the cuffs and patted him down, but he didn't have a gun.

"You're one of them guys we tried to kill, ain't you?" the man said, finally realizing who Frankie was.

"First prize for the man in the handcuffs," said Frankie, and opening the rear door of the pickup, bungled the man in.

"Stay there and behave. If you don't, I'll kill you, understand?" The man nodded vigorously. Satisfied the man was secure, he put his gun away and walked over to Sam. "Okay, well, that went well enough," said Frankie. "What now?" Sam handed Frankie a pair of plastic gloves. You follow me in their truck. I'll try to find somewhere we can interrogate them. Frankie went around the truck, got in the driving seat. The truck's engine was still running. He waited for Sam's car to maneuver in front of him, then followed it. At the end of the service road, Sam turned left.

It wasn't long before they got to an area where trees flanked both sides of the road, with a lake on the left. Sam took a left on to a dirt rack and drove for a good few minutes until they reached a clearing by the lakeside. Sam stopped his car, got out, and had a look around. Frankie got out of the truck and waited. The only sounds were the screeching of birds and some strange other animal noises. The heat was oppressive, flies everywhere. Sam walked to the water's edge and looked around. Nodding to himself, he walked back.

"Looks reasonably private Frankie," said Sam, taking a silencer out of his trouser pocket and fixing on to his Glock 22. Frankie followed Sam's lead and attached a moderator to his gun. The act wasn't lost on the two captured men. Sam and Frankie opened the rear doors of their respective vehicles.

"Out," said Sam to the man sat in the rear of his Lincoln. The man didn't move. Sam grabbed the man by the collar, dragged him out and pushed him down on to the floor. The one in the back of the truck got out without the need to be told. He looked at Frankie, who pointed at the floor, near to the first man. He sat on the floor awkwardly by his partner's side.

Sam moved to the rear of the truck, pulled down the tailgate, reached in the back, and brought out a bag. It contained two handguns and some ammunition. He walked to the edge of the lake, swung the bag and threw it out as far as he could out into the lake. He went back to the truck and retrieved an oblong bag. Inside it was a case which Sam opened to reveal a deconstructed modular rifle, silencer and telescopic sight.

"Well, looky here," said Sam. Frankie walked over and took a closer look.

"That's a Nemesis," he said. "Sniper's modular rifle. No doubt the one this guy used to try to kill us," Sam looked at Frankie and raised his eyebrows.

"Did a stint as a sniper in Iraq, part of my Special Forces training."

"Figures," said Sam. "What do we do with it Frankie?"

"Keep it. Might come in handy." Frankie reached further back into the truck, took out a small shoulder bag, "Look, here's the ammunition."

"Okay," said Sam, and walking over to his car, popped the trunk, took out a large metal tool case it and gestured for Frankie to put the rifle in the trunk. Frankie closed the rifle case, grabbed hold of the bag of ammunition, and dropped both items in the trunk of Sam's car. Sam closed the trunk lid and walked across to where the men were sitting and placed the toolbox on the ground. "Keep them covered while I look for some ID."

Frankie took out his handgun and moved so he was behind both men. "Any of these two try anything, don't hesitate, shoot." Sam said. He made the driver stand up, went through his jean pockets, and emptied them. He did the same with the second man.

Then he went to the truck to look for any jackets or other of the men's belongings. He threw two jean jackets and two holdall bags on the floor then went through those. Satisfied he had all he needed, he threw the men's belongings back into the truck, along with the bags.

"Okay, so we have one Charles A Tuffin."

"Abner," said smaller man, "my middle name's Abner, I hate the name Charles."

"Okay, Abner it is. And one Larson Stipp. So, who's the big dog in this two-man team?"

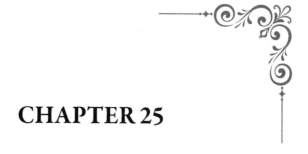

CHAPTER 25

"He's the boss," said Abner, nodding towards Stipp.

"Shut your fat mouth, you idiot!" Larson Stipp yelled at his partner. Randazzo looked at Frankie and smiled, then spoke to the two men.

"Okay, so here's the rules. I'll ask you questions and if I don't believe the answers, you'll be punished. See, I don't have all the sophisticated drugs you used on me to make me talk, so we're going to have to use old-fashioned methods."

"Don't know what you're talking about," said Larson Stipp, "we ain't never seen you before."

"Way too late for that, my friend," said Frankie, "your partner here already blew it. Now what was it he said, oh yeah, 'you one of them guys we tried to kill, aren't you?'" Larson Stipp looked at his partner and shook his head. Sam went over to his toolbox and took out a pair of pliers and a hammer. He went behind Larson Stipp and got the man's little finger of his left hand in the jaws of the pliers. He bent the finger back until Stipp yelled. Leaning over Stipp's shoulder, Sam said in a calm voice.

"I'm going to begin by breaking one of your fingers, and I'll repeat the process every time I don't like the answer you give. There was a cracking noise, and Larson Stipp screamed in agony. A bird screeched back as if responding to the scream. Larson Stipp cursed.

"You vicious bastard, fuckin animal." Then Stipp bent his head to hide his sobs. Most of the color had drained out of Abner's face.

"We got all day, my friends," said Sam, "so we can either make this long, drawn out and very painful, or you can just tell me the truth. Let's start again. Besides trying to kill us the other day, you're also the two guys who kidnapped me, right? Either of you can answer."

"Yes, we are," said Abner Tuffin wearily. Stipp yelled.

"I told you. Keep that big fat trap of yours shut!"

"What's the point Lars? They know anyway." Stipp had no reply to that and hung his head.

"I think you've probably figured out the next question. Who's pulling the strings here, who's giving the orders? And why do they want us dead? Have a think about the consequences of lying before you answer." Both men were silent. "Okay, time's up, time to answer." Sam said. Neither man spoke. Sam sighed and got his pliers out of the toolbox again, went round the back of Abner Tuffin and fixed the pliers on one of Abner's little fingers and began to bend his little finger backwards. Abner's face contorted, and he started to make a keening noise.

"Stop!" said Larson Stipp. "I'll tell you as much as we know, but it ain't that much, really." Sam released Abner's little finger. "We, that is, me and Abner. Originally, we were both in the services. We didn't really know each other back then, but we both got sheep dipped by the FBI. You heard of sheep dipping, I guess?"

"I have," said Sam, looking at Frankie, who had his eyebrows raised a quizzical look on his face. "Later," Sam said. Frankie nodded. "So, you were both recruited by the FBI?"

"Yeah, they put us together. Look, they find out I told you any of this, I'm dead, we're dead."

"No reason it would get back to them if you're being straight with us" Larson frowned and nodded.

"See, we never did none of the real complicated stuff. Mostly surveillance and so on. They called us field operatives, but we were really just low-level grunts. We had to infiltrate groups sometimes, they said to find out what their plans or intentions were, but mostly it was to stir 'em up, agitate, feed them information and so on. The FBI told us how to trick these groups, get them to make plans to do something the Feds could get them on. Or record them saying or planning something radical. They even sent us to South America, and a couple of places in the Caribbean."

Most of the time, we were stumbling around in the dark. We were never really given the full picture. They never told us the detail, just told us what to do, who our targets were. We did do the occasional hit job. Always told it was justified, that we were protecting our national security, all that sorta bullshit.

"We get the picture, so fast forward," said Sam.

"Okay, so we both decided to leave the service, but they never really let you leave. I'd always wanted to go back to some sort of farming. I grew up on a farm, Abner wanted out as well, so we left. We got as far as getting a job on a ranch in Tennessee, but pretty soon we were contacted by a guy who said his name was Bentley, and he had a job for us. Good pay short contract. The job turned out to be kidnapping you and finding out all you knew about a Mrs. Fairman and the Jordan family."

"Do you know why he wanted this information? Frankie asked.

"No, like I said, we were told what to do, not why," Stipp replied

"This Bentley guy, where did he operate from?" asked Randazzo

"He has an office in Athens, Huntsville, near the university. We can tell you where the office is and the phone number he gave us. He'd likely know more than us, but I'm sure he ain't the main man in this. He's just a coupla rungs higher up the ladder than us."

"You ever hear the name Gerald Jordan mentioned?" asked Frankie

"Nope. Like I said, we're just told what to do. Bentley got good and mad when he found out we hadn't killed you after the kidnap. Sent us to Naples to finish the job." Stipp looked at Sam, then at Frankie.

"Look, wasn't nothing personal, just a job." Frankie laughed, looked at Sam, and shook his head.

"You thought you'd killed us but found out pretty quick you hadn't. How'd you find out so soon?" asked Sam.

"Bentley must have someone watching you. He called us to say we'd screwed up again and told us to make it right or else."

"So, when he finds out the situation now, what's he likely to do?"

"He'll send someone to kill us. When you grabbed us back there, we were on our way back to Huntsville to grab some of our personal shit, some rainy-day money we got stashed away, then skedaddle. Get as far away from Alabama as we could. Mexico maybe." Stipp paused, then added. "Now we're screwed, well and truly screwed."

"Anything you want to add to what your pal just told us?" Sam asked Abner Tuffin. Abner looked at Sam and shook his head.

"What Lars told you is the truth. Like he says, we're screwed six ways to Sunday."

"What you gonna do with us?" said Larson Stipp. "I don't want to go to no jail. That wouldn't stop our employer from having us killed. I'd rather you just shot me here and now."

"Can I have a word, Sam?" Frankie asked, nodding his head towards the far side of the clearing. They both walked away from the two prisoners, spoke in low voices for a while, Sam nodded, and they walked back.

"Okay, here's the deal," said Frankie. "We all drive to Alabama. When we get there, you, Stipp, are going to call this Mr. Bentley and arrange to meet up with him."

"That's kinda dangerous in the circumstances. Why would I do that?"

"The alternative is we take you in to the cops in Naples. We'll start with attempted murder, you can take your chances from there, your choice," said Sam. Stipp thought for a while then spoke.

"If we take you to Bentley, what happens afterwards?"

"Well, providing Frankie and I are still, how can I put it, still in charge of the situation, then you go free." Stipp turned to look at his partner.

"Abner?"

"I couldn't do jail time Lars. Like you said, they'd sure as hell have us killed inside. So yeah, I say we take 'em to Bentley."

Frankie and Sam discussed the problem of having three vehicles to drive to Alabama. Frankie came up with a workable solution.

"We leave my Jeep where it is, drive their truck and pick my jeep up on the way back."

"Yep, that works. I doubt anyone's going to bother with it."

"Okay Sam, so you take Stipp in the back of your car, hands shackled together, plus maybe another restraint shackling him to the rear door furthest away from you. I do the same with Abner and follow you in their truck."

"And what do we do when we arrive in Huntsville," Sam said.

"We can figure that out on the way. That sniper rifle's given me an idea."

Before they set off, Frankie made a splint for Stipp's broken finger from small pieces of twigs and some tape from Sam's toolbox.

The journey was long and tedious. Sam didn't want to converse with Stipp, so he listened to some radio chat shows alternating with country music stations. Stipp slept most of the way. Frankie, on the other hand, was pumping Abner for information on Huntsville and began to make a plan.

Both prisoners kept to the rules and two rest stops and eleven hours later at 3:00. a.m., they started to see signs for Huntsville Alabama I -72, they parked in the next rest stop. Sam got out and walked over to Frankie, who'd got out of the truck to stretch his legs. They discussed tactics.

There was the option of sleeping at Stipp's place, but Sam thought there were too many logistical problems regarding the security of their two prisoners, not just for Frankie and Sam's sake, but for the two prisoners themselves. Sam pointed out that Bentley might well have sent men to stake Stipp's place out. So, he and Frankie decided they'd all sleep in the cars at the rest stop. Both of their charges were duly secured in the back of their respective vehicles. Frankie and Sam slept in the driving seats.

Early the next morning, Sam and Frankie took it in turns to use the restrooms then supervised Stipp and Tuffin while they used the restrooms. No one questioned why the two men in cuffs were being escorted in and out of the restroom area. One man looked as if he was going to ask Sam something, but averted his eyes and scurried off when Sam gave him the hard stare.

With their charges back safely cuffed and back in the vehicles, Sam went to get some take away coffees and doughnuts from the gas station shop and gave some to Abner and Lars. While their prisoners were eating their breakfast, Frankie and Sam stood some way from the cars and discussed Frankie's plan.

"Okay, let's have it."

"This Bentley guy is ruthless, as we know. These men don't seem to have any doubt that Bentley will have them killed as soon as he can find them. But I think we can use that to our advantage. It's risky, but anything will be. And there's no saying this Bentley guy will go for it, but this is what I worked out with the help of Abner."

"He tells me there's a disused airfield to the south of Huntsville called Ringway. It's surrounded by trees so nice and private. He reckons Bentley would know it or could find out easily enough where it is. There's a sort of ring road around the airport with a couple of dirt roads at each end leading in and out of the airfield, one road from the south and one from the north. We go there now, and you get Stipp to call Bentley, then he hands the phone to you. You say you want to meet.

"And why would he agree to that?"

"I think he will. You tell him you have the two goons who kidnapped you, then tried to kill us both. You want to exchange them for information on what this is all about."

"Or what?"

"You say if he doesn't agree, you'll turn them over to the authorities. Maybe he wouldn't want that. The FBI don't like investigations into their unofficial activities or whatever this is."

"And what if he asks about you?"

"Those two shot me. I'm badly injured, but not dead. You say if they'd have killed me, you'd have killed Stipp and Tufin, but you think this is a better option, because Stipp and Tuffin say you, Bentley, will kill them if you get your hands on them, anyway. So, you'd be happy enough with that, etc., plus you get to know what's going on. I mean, you're going to have to play it by ear. It's the best I can do. Maybe he'll buy it maybe he won't?"

"When and how?"

"Okay, well we drive to this airfield now, make sure it's as Tuffin says it is, then we, that is Stipp, calls him, then hands the phone to you and you do your stuff. Say you're there already and make a time to meet."

"Surely he'll realize it's a setup?"

"I guess he would. The alternative is we get there and tell him we're about an hour and a half away, so give him time to arrange a nice little surprise for us?

"Hmm. I still don't think he'll fall for it, but can't think of another angle, so what's to lose by trying?"

"You might say something about why they're coming after you, that maybe they've got the wrong guy, something like that..."

"And what if he doesn't agree to meet?"

"We go back to the drawing board. Another thought. Tell hm you'll be armed, and if you see anyone with him, you'll leave and take his two pet thugs with you."

"Hmm," Sam thought for a couple of minutes. "Hard for this Bentley guy to resist, even if he smells a rat, which he will."

"I'm banking on his desire to kill you, overcomes too much caution."

"Okay, and I assume we go early, so you can get into position with that rifle?"

"Yep, and I'm going to need your field glasses as well."

"Okay, anything else?"

"Well, ideally, I'd like to have some time to calibrate the rifle sights, but I'm just going to wing it. The targets won't be that small."

"Do we have a fallback plan?"

"Nope, but let's see if he goes for it. He has to believe I'm badly injured. If he doesn't believe that...."

"Okay, let's see if he takes the bait. But do me a big favor. If you have to shoot Bentley, don't kill him. I need him alive, okay?"

"Understood."

CHAPTER 26

S am went back to his car, sat in the driver's seat and turned around
to speak to Larson Stipp who was still cuffed and sitting in the
back. It took a while to convince him it was in his and his partner's
interests to make the call.

"So, we go to meet Bentley like two sacrificial lambs? What's to
stop him blowing our heads off? Or leastways getting someone else to
shoot us. We'll be like sitting ducks out there in the open. You too,
for that matter. It's a crazy plan." Sam sighed. He found it hard to
argue when it was put like that, and he too began to have some doubts.
Frankie stood at the open car door, listening to the conversation and
saying nothing.

"Look, Frankie here's going to be in place and watching. He's going
to know if Bentley sends some guys ahead to set a trap. That's the reason
we're going to get there before we call him. Steal a march on the guy,
give Frankie time to get set up well before Bentley gets anything set up
himself. But for this to work, we have to convince Bentley that you shot
Frankie, and he's badly injured and in hospital or something." Stipp said
nothing but was obviously processing what he'd just be told. Randazzo
continued. "I can take care of any moves Bentley makes at the meet, and
Frankie will deal with any other threats."

"Bentley's smart, he ain't no pushover," Stipp replied, "Why not
just have Frankie here kill Bentley as soon as he shows up?"

"Because I have to know. I need to find out the whole story. Who
wants me dead and why? I won't settle for anything less. We kill Bentley

and they'll just have someone else take his place. You know that as well as I do. And think about it my friend, you and your pal here have just as much to lose as we do." Stipp shook his head slowly, then seem to come to a decision.

"Okay....., I guess you're right. You spoke with Abner about this?"

"No, but he normally lets you make the decisions, don't he?"

"Yeah, he does. Let's get to this airfield and make the call."

They reached the old airport in less than an hour and found the southern dirt track that led directly into the disused airfield. The runways were still discernable despite the parched grass, weeds and small bushes that strove to take back the land to its original state. The perimeter was bordered by large trees and bushes which screened it from the road, making it an ideal meeting place for their purposes. Sam and Frankie got out of their respective vehicles and looked around.

"Okay, looks ideal, better than I'd hoped. Let's go find somewhere to park your Lincoln out of sight. I'll follow you." Frankie followed Sam's car out of the dirt road on to the road that circled the old airport. Sam found a discreet place to park about a mile away on a side road off the Airport Road. He got out, popped the trunk and transferred the rifle case and binoculars to the rear of the truck, then let Stipp out of the back and told him to get into the truck. Frankie drove them all back to the disused airport and parked up, facing north and where the truck could be seen by anyone entering the airport grounds from the north entrance. They all got out.

"Okay Stipp, time to make that call," said Sam and handed Stipp's cell back to him. He looked at the cell phone but didn't take it.

"Let us both out of these cuffs first?"

"No, not yet. After this is over, we give you back your truck and let you and Tuffin go free, but until then, you stay shackled. Don't forget Stipp, you and your buddy here tried to murder me and Frankie. Most guys would kill you for that, so consider yourselves very lucky." Stipp looked at Tuffin, then back at Sam, nodded and took the cell out of Sam's hand. He made the call.

"Yeah, Larson here Mr. Bentley. Yeah, Larsson Stipp" Stipp raised his eyes to heaven. "Yeah, we're in Huntsville, well near Huntsville.... Yeah, well, we're not able to do that, we're what you might call, compromised...Yeah, one of the guys you sent us to kill. He wants to meet up with you," said Stipp. "Okay, I'll put him on." Stipp handed his cell to Sam.

"Sam Randazzo."

"Mr. Randazzo, how can I help you?"

"Maybe we can help each other?"

"Really, how so?"

"I have your two thugs here in handcuffs. You can have them back in exchange for information." Bentley laughed derisively.

"What makes you think I want them back?"

"Okay, in that case, I'll hand them over to the authorities, along with what information I know about them and you, and let things take their course. Maybe they'll come looking for you? I certainly will, and I won't rest until I find you and kill you."

"I don't respond well to threats, Mr. Randazzo. And you're playing well out of your league."

"Okay, have it your way."

"Hold on, not so fast. I'm thinking... You said I have, not we have. Where's your partner?"

"In hospital. Your two goons tried to kill us again, and they nearly succeeded this time. My partner got shot. They think he'll recover, but he ain't in great shape."

"Oh, I'm real sorry to hear that, Mr. Randazzo."

"Course you are. So yes or no, I ain't wasting any more of my time. I have other options. I'm still wondering if I should turn the whole thing over to the authorities, anyway. Let them deal with it. Trouble is, I think you'd just disappear. These men say you're with the FBI. Are you?" Bentley was silent for a few beats, then spoke.

"I'll need to bring someone with me."

"I see anyone else in the vicinity and I leave and take your two thugs with me and go to the authorities." Bentley was silent again, then spoke.

"Where and when?"

"You know the old disused Huntsville airport?"

"I believe I do. When?"

"An hour from now. Come in through the north entrance and come alone. Like I say, I see anyone else with you and I leave."

"You there now?"

"I am, why?"

"I can probably get there in less than an hour, that's all. Is that a problem for you?

"No."

"And I'll be on my own but armed, so any tricks...."

"Likewise, Bentley, likewise." Sam cut the line and pocketed Stipp's cell.

"He take the bait?" asked Frankie

"On the face of it, yeah. Says he'll be here in less than an hour, probably." "You think he bought the bit about me being in hospital?"

"Hard to say, could be he did?"

"Hmm," said Frankie and turned to Stipp.

"How long to get from Bentley's office to here, d'you think?"

"'Bout half an hour I guess." Stipp replied. Frankie looked at his watch.

"I'd better get set up. Where are you going to be Sam?"

"Just here, back of the truck. I'll have Stipp and Tuffin standing in front of the truck, but I need to keep an eye on the road here, just in case Bentley comes sneaking in this way."

"And if he does?"

"I start shooting and you come and join in."

"Okay," said Frankie and taking the rifle case and binoculars, walked into the undergrowth behind where they were, to find a good spot to lie in wait. Ten minutes later, he came out and wandered back over to the truck.

"Found a good place where I can see pretty well everything on the airfield. You set up here, Sam?"

"Yup, Stipp and Tuffin are non too happy about this. Can't say I'm thrilled either. We're sitting ducks if he decides to send a sniper."

"Maybe move those two into the cab of the truck. They'll have some protection that way. Or we can call this off, get in the truck and leave, think of another way."

"Yeah, I know, but I can't think of another way, can you Frankie?"

"Not without involving the authorities."

"How long to Bentley arriving now, d'you think?"

"Been twenty minutes or so since the call, so another ten minutes or more, depending."

"Okay Frankie, let's take our chances then. I'll do like you say and go move the men inside the truck."

When Frankie thought about it later, he couldn't remember if he heard it or saw it first. He'd just turned round to walk back to his hiding place when something caught his attention just before he'd turned around. He stopped, looked back and saw what looked like a buzzard flying high in the sky over the airport, then he heard the noise. Sam was also looking skywards.

Frankie grabbed at Sam's shirt and pulled him with him as he ran for the tree cover. Sam resisted initially.

"What the.... Frankie?"

"Sam... now!" said Frankie, and they both ran the short distance to the tree line and ducked as they ran into the cover of the bushes. Sam was a second or two behind Frankie, still unsure of what was happening, but then he heard the unmistakable sound of machine gun fire. He dived into the bushes and rolled over. He lay alongside Frankie as they looked out through the bushes and long grass.

The airfield in front of the truck was being strafed by a hail of bullets, which, split seconds later, tore into the front of the truck. Stipp and Tufin didn't stand a chance. By the time they'd realized what was happening, they were cut to ribbons in a hail of bullets. Then the truck exploded into a fireball.

"Christ almighty! They must have hit the gas tank or a fuel pipe. Come on Sam, we've got to get out of here, they'll start on this area next." They heard the noise of the drone change slightly as it wheeled around to select a new target area. They ran through the undergrowth, hampered by the long grass, stumbling and zig zagging around the trees, their arms and faces whipped by the lower branches as they desperately tried to reach the road. Behind them, the bullets started to rip through the tree line just yards away.

They came to a low wall, leaped over and lay behind it panting for air. They were shielded from the bullets for now.

"What on earth was that?!" Sam said as soon as he could speak.

"A drone, a quad copter with a machine gun. I didn't know they were that advanced, but if anyone's going to have access to weapons like that, it would be the FBI." The firing was getting closer, then suddenly stopped. Sam looked at Frankie.

"Those drones have a limited payload, so probably used up all their fire power for now. It'll need to land to be re-armed."

"Come on then, let's get to my car and get the hell out of here." A few minutes later, they got to where they'd parked Sam's Lincoln. Both men took out their side arms and looked around to make sure they weren't walking into another trap. Satisfied they weren't, they got in the Lincoln and drove off.

"Any ideas about what we do next?" asked Frankie

"I do. You still got Bentley's office address?"

"Yes, it's on my cell."

"Put it in your cell GPS. I've had enough of this guy." Frankie did as Sam asked.

"Do we have a plan?" he asked.

"No, no plan, we use our instinct. We go to his office and see if he's there, and work something out as we go along. You okay with that?"

"I am," said Frankie."

"If he is there, it's going to get rough."

They arrived at the suite of offices in Athens, Huntsville, some forty minutes later and found a place to park around the corner. Sam switched off the engine.

"How are we going to do this?"

"Nothing fancy, just find his office and, if necessary, kick the door in. Any opposition we shoot first, ask questions later... what?" Frankie reached in his pocket, took out some picks and dangled them in front of Sam. "Okay, well, maybe we can be a bit more subtle." Frankie smiled, put the picks back in his pocket, un-holstered his Glock 19, and checked it out.

"Let's go," he said. They both exited the car and walked around the corner to the door of the office block. They were in luck and a man who was just exiting kept the door open for them to pass through. Frankie gave him a cheery little wave of thanks.

"Pays to look respectable." Sam said as they walked into the lobby, looking at Frankie's shorts and smiling.

"I think it was more to do with my stylishly casual look." Frankie replied. They both donned plastic gloves.

"These look like temporary office," Sam said, looking at the sign on the wall 'Offices to Rent by the Month'. "Interesting. What did Stipp say, third floor?"

"Yes, third floor, second door on the right as you come out of the elevator."

They arrived on the third floor and located the office door. No name or indication of who occupied the office. They both took out their guns. Sam knocked, no response. He waited and knocked again, harder. Still no response. Frankie moved to the door and took out his picks. It took him less than a minute to open the door.

Once inside, they locked the door and cleared the rooms, two small ante rooms and rest room, then came back to the main office. Frankie looked around the place. There was a large desk and chair, a filing cabinet, another smaller desk with a desktop computer on it and a printer-scanner.

"Spartan, I think is the appropriate description," he said. "This is a token office, just somewhere to meet people in private when he's in town. I bet they have lots of offices like this in different parts of the country."

Sam searched the filing cabinet, and Frankie took the desk drawers. Apart from one desk drawer, no others were locked, nor was the filing cabinet, which was empty, other than the drawer containing a bottle of Chivas Regal and four glasses. Sam took out the bottle, two of the glasses, and put them on the desk.

Frankie went to work on the locked drawer and soon had it open. There was one thick manilla file. He put it on the desktop and opened it. Inside was a sheaf of document and photographs. Sam spread the photographs on the desk. They were mainly shots of Sam at the various film locations, also some of Frankie. Sam and Frankie each quickly read through the documents.

"Chapter and verse on each of us. Lots of background stuff even I'd forgotten," said Sam. "They've certainly been doing their homework on us, but why for Chissakes?" He shook his head, grabbed the bottle of Chivas Regal and poured a couple of fingers into each tumbler. Frankie picked his drink up. They chinked glasses.

"Wishing you all the bad luck in the world, Mr. Bentley," said Frankie

"Amen to that," Sam replied, and they both drank their scotch in one gulp. Just as they put their glasses down, they heard noises in the corridor. Sam took out his gun and went round the desk to sit in the chair behind it, his gun pointed at the doorway. Frankie quickly moved to the side of the office door, flattened himself against the wall, took out his gun and held it by his leg. Someone unlocked the door, and it opened. Frankie was now hidden behind the open door.

"What the....?"

"Come in. Mr. Bentley, I assume. And bring your friends in with you." Frankie got the message, So that's at least three of them.... He readied himself, then realized Bentley would see the two glasses on the desk, shit! Frankie didn't know who shot first, but he heaved at the door to push the men off balance, then moved into the room backwards, shooting in their general direction before he could actually see anyone.

In his side vison, he could see Sam shooting from behind the desk as he backed up to get a better shot. He saw one of the men was down. Frankie pulled the trigger three times in quick succession at one of the other men. The man fell to the floor on his knees, then collapsed sideways. That left one man standing. He was noticeably older than the two men. He had his gun in two hands pointing forwards, but realized he was in big trouble. He kept turning to quickly look at Frankie, then forwards at where Sam had been sitting.

Sam had been crouched behind the desk, but now slowly emerged, pointing his gun at him. The man knew he had nowhere to go, lowered his gun, then let it fall to the floor.

"Mr. Bentley, meet my partner, Mr. Armstrong."

"Fuck you." Bentley spat out the words. "You morons don't know how much trouble you're in." Sam came around the desk and stood in front of Bentley and punched him hard in the solar plexus. Despite his obvious size and strength, Bentley doubled. Sam kicked his legs from under him, then kneeled down and put his gun to Bentley's head.

"Just give me any excuse to shoot you here and now Bentley. Now get up and do what you're told or die here now. I don't give a shit either way." Bentley slowly got to his feet.

"Turn round and face front. We're going to walk out of here. Do exactly as I say. If I even think you're going to try to make a break for it, I'll shoot you and so will Frankie here. Got it?" Bentley remained silent. Sam moved round him and stuck his gun under Bentley's chin with some force. Bentley's head was forced back. "I said, got it?"

"I got it," said Bentley in a strangled voice. Sam took the pistol away, got Bentley by the arm, and walked them both towards the open door.

"Come on, Frankie and grab that file. We'd better scoot before the cops arrive. I'll walk behind him, you walk by his right-hand side. If he makes one wrong move, don't hesitate, shoot the bastard."

"Be my pleasure," said Frankie, going to the door and scanning the corridor. "Clear," he said, turned, grabbed Bentley by his upper arm and marched him out of the room towards the elevator. Sam brought up the rear.

CHAPTER 27

They got to where the Lincoln was parked, and Sam unlocked the car. With Frankie still covering Bentley, Sam reached in, took out a spare pair of cuffs from the glove compartment, pushed Bentley up against the car and cuffed his wrists behind him.

"Keep your gun ready while I frisk him," Sam said as he quickly patted Bentley down and searched his pockets. He retrieved a wallet from Bentley's inside jacket pocket, then opening the rear door, bungled Bentley into the back seat. They got under way and Frankie navigated while Sam drove and soon, they were on the I-565 going west then on towards the I-65 Southwards. Once they were well clear of the area, Sam let out a long sigh.

"Anything interesting in that wallet?" he asked.

"A driving license and some dollars. Seems our friend's real name is James Royce, born in Nebraska in 1960," said Frankie. "Nothing much more than that."

"Royce, calls himself Bentley.... that checks out," said Sam smiling wryly. "On another day I'd find that amusing." Frankie put the wallet in his shorts pocket.

"That's some mess we left back there."

"Sure is man, the local cops will be going crazy. A truck strafed by bullets at the old airfield, then blown up, with two burnt bodies shot to bits in it. Two more people shot to death in a rented office in Athens."

"What d'you reckon the chances are of connecting us to either of those incidents?"

"Well, you got the file, so no other paperwork there to connect us, as far as we could see. The cops will probably find a street video of us near the offices," Sam said, "but they won't know who we are. We'll just be a couple of guys mixed with all the other folks on the street. But if they have video of us going in or coming out of those offices, especially coming out with bozo in the back here, then they'll really start trying to identify who we are. It's anyone's guess. I'd say it's fifty fifty."

"Will the FBI know about us? Assuming Bentley's with the FBI, that is?"

"Depends. This seems to me like something off the grid, maybe. I mean, why would the Bureau be interested in me, or us? Something don't ring true here. We need to find out what this is all about and how it connects back to Billy Fairman."

"Have you any ideas on how we find out?"

"First opportunity we get, we need to interrogate Bentley," a snort of derision emanated from the back of the car, "but let's get plenty of distance between us and Huntsville first." They drove for another two and a half hours before turning into TJ's Travel Center and Truck Stop. Sam drove slowly through the parking lot, past the gas pumps and on past the trucks and parked up by a large patch of sun scorched grass, well away from the main site and screened by a wooden fence. Sam switched off the engine, then he and Frankie turned in their seats to face Bentley. Sam spoke.

"Okay, Bentley, or Royce, whatever your name is. Time for some straight talking. It seems obvious from your use of that very advanced armed drone back there that you're part of some government organization. Even the most sophisticated terrorist cells are unlikely to have access to that sort of equipment, at least in the US. So, are you with the FBI, yes or no.?" Bentley smiled as if Sam had asked a really dumb question.

"Those drones are something else, ain't they? And yes, I'm an FBI Field Officer. Been with the Bureau for over twenty-five years now."

Sam looked at Frankie and raised his eyebrows. "Look fellas," Bentley continued, "I ain't got nothing to hide, so forget about the thumb screws, okay? It's not that I'm afraid, hardly. I was a Navy Seal before I joined the Bureau and been in some real tight spots, so you two don't bother me. In fact, I almost feel sorry for you. You two gone and stepped in one big pile of doodoo."

"Okay. Well, seeing you're feeling so sorry for us, perhaps you'll tell us what this is all about. Why was I targeted, and then Frankie here as well?"

"You stumbled into something. Someone who thought you might expose something damaging to them."

"I think we guessed that much. Who is it and what did we nearly stumble into?" Bentley smiled.

"Let's just say you represented a potential threat. The guy's very powerful and paranoid."

"So, why is the FBI involved?"

"The FBI isn't involved, not directly." Sam looked at Frankie, who raised his eyebrows.

"This guy is so powerful, he can use the FBI as his private enforcers and assassins?" said Frankie

"Come on, you know how it works. Look, just let me go, stay away from Mrs. Fairman and the Jordans. Maybe I can convince the guy you're not a danger to him."

"Oh yeah, that sounds nice. What do you think Frankie, shall we just promise to be good boys and hope the nice man will stop trying to kill us?" Frankie laughed.

"Yeah right.... Here's our counter-offer," said Frankie, "you tell us who this guy is, and we'll put a good word in for you with the authorities when we hand you over."

"Hmm. Let me consider that. Look, I really need a piss," said Bentley, squirming and looking uncomfortable. "I can't think straight. No one can see me if I stand over there by that tree." Sam looked and scanned the immediate area, then got out and opened the rear door of the car. Frankie got out and went round the car to stand beside Sam.

"Out, and don't try anything." Bentley got out.

"I need you to take these off, or at least cuff me at the front."

"Frankie," said Sam, "cover him while I change the cuffs over." Frankie stood behind Bentley with his Glock held discreetly by his side. Sam undid the cuffs. Bentley put his hands in front of him and rubbed his wrists. Frankie glanced away briefly as a squirrel jumped down from a tree on to the grass, then fast as greased lighting, in one fluid movement, Bentley pushed Sam over, bent down sideways, took a gun out of an ankle holster and turned to shoot Frankie. Frankie had gone on to auto pilot and a split second before Bentley pulled the trigger, Frankie shot the man square in the chest.

"Holy Christ!" said Sam as he scrambled to stand up straight. He looked down at Bentley's collapsed body. Frankie moved forwards, leaned down and picked up the little gun.

"Sig P365," he said, more to himself than to Sam.

"Bit late to be learning that lesson," said Sam, "I messed up and it coulda cost us our lives."

"Don't beat yourself up about it Sam, understandable in the circumstances," he said as he slid the small pistol into his shorts pocket. He bent down and kneeled by the body. Bentley's face suddenly contorted, and his lips moved. "He's still alive," said Frankie and bent his head to hear what Bentley was saying. Sam had his cell in his hand.

"Do I call 911?" In answer, Frankie held up his hand to signal wait, then Bentley's head rolled sideways. Frankie checked his neck for a pulse.

"He's gone," said Frankie and closed Bentley's eyelids with his fingers, then stood up.

"He say anything useful?"

"I think he said, 'you were fast' then, I don't know. I'll swear he mumbled something like, 'this is no way to live' least think that was it." Sam laughed.

"Groucho's last words. My pop was always quoting that kinda stuff. Bentley sure was a comedian. Lord knows what we do now."

"Sorry Sam, I had no choice, he'd have killed me for sure. Now we've lost our best chance of finding out what this is all about."

"It's hardly your fault Frankie, it's mine. I fell for it, you had no choice."

"So, where do we go from here?"

"We take a leaf out of the sleuthing detection manual, chapter one, line one, follow the money. These things are always about money and power," said Sam, "They go together like peaches and cream?" Frankie answered, replied,

"What about sex?"

"Oh, that comes as an automatic bonus." Sam replied. Frankie smiled,

"I really must get me a copy of that sleuthing manual. But on a more urgent note, what the hell do we do with Bentley's body?"

Sam walked to the end of the fence and looked around. He turned back to Frankie.

"No one's rushing over. Let's get him in the trunk. I've got an old towel in there, should save my trunk carpet from getting too stained with his blood." Frankie took the legs, Sam the arms and they tucked Bentley's body into the trunk, then Frankie went over to where a large bloodstain was left on the dry ground where Bentley had collapsed. He used his foot to cover it with dirt and dust from the immediate area. That done, they had one final look around, then got in the Lincoln and they drove off.

"Going to be interesting trying to get his body out of there when rigor sets in, in a couple of hours."

"Shit, hadn't thought of that."

"Couldn't leave him there though, so.... Any ideas about where to dump his body?"

"Don't have a clue, but we can plan as we drive south. And don't forget, we've got to stop to collect your car."

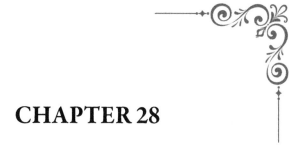

CHAPTER 28

The journey took them back down the I-75 until they reached the truck stop where they'd left Frankie's jeep. They both got out and looked at each other.

"The lake!"

"Great minds, Sam." Think we can find it again?"

"A breeze," he replied, "get back in." They found the service road that led to the same dirt track road and drove along it until the lake appeared on the left. They turned off the road and along the dirt track to the same clearing by the water. Getting out of the car, they looked around.

"You got any rope?" asked Frankie.

"Nope."

"We could go back to the truck stop and buy some, but then that gets complicated. Can't see any suitable sized rocks around here and even if we got some rope and boulders, how would we get him out to the deep water? I think we're over complicating things. Let's just dump the body in the trees, as far out of sight as possible. He's got no ID on him, and anyway, around here, the critters are going to find him soon enough. There's nothing to link his body with us, is there?" Sam gave Frankie's suggestion some consideration.

"You're right Frankie, no witnesses. No one knows we killed him. Some of his buddies in the Bureau might know he was after us, but their difficulty would be that he was working this one unofficially. They couldn't admit to that without making big trouble for themselves. I think we should go with your suggestion, keep it simple. When I get back, I'll arrange to have my trunk sanitized, just in case. Come on, let's his body out."

Rigor mortis had set in, and Bentley wasn't a small man. They struggled but managed to get Bentley's body out of the trunk. At Frankie's suggestion they stripped off most of his clothes, bungled them back into the trunk to be disposed of later, then carried Bentley's body a long way into the trees, covering it up with some leaves and twigs.

"You think we should say a few words?" asked Frankie

"Yeah, I do. Bye asshole."

"Amen," said Frankie solemnly, then they both convulsed, laughing. They covered his body with more leaves and whatever they could find, more branches, more twigs and leaves. "I can't see anyone coming across his body unless they were looking for it."

"Yeah, and with a bit of luck, it will be partially eaten, or fully decomposed before anyone finds it." They got back in the car and drove back to the truck stop to collect Frankie's Jeep, then got back on to the I-75 for the long drive south back to Naples. They stopped off at another truck stop well south of their last stop and found a dumpster in which to dispose of Bentley's clothes.

Back home, both men caught up with their own private lives, whilst keeping in contact with each other. Sam went to visit Clive on the film set, which had moved back to Naples for some final short sequences. Clive explained they were more or less finished in the locality and would be leaving for Miami in the next couple of days to continue filming there. And so, they wouldn't need their security services any longer. Sam said he'd send his bill and told Clive he and Frankie would like to come and see him the next day to tidy up one of two loose ends. Clive said that wouldn't be a problem.

"I'll be working from the shop in the mall for the next day or so, so you'll know where to find me."

That evening, Frankie took Daisy out for a meal at Cibao. She quizzed him about his trip to Alabama, and much as he hated doing it, he carefully avoided mentioning the more gruesome aspects of his experiences in the last few days. He realized he wasn't really fooling Daisy, but she didn't push him on it. He also knew he would have to come clean eventually, but until things were brought to a conclusion, he felt it would be unwise to tell Daisy the whole story. He just hoped she wouldn't be too pissed with him when he eventually told her all.

Both he and Sam monitored the news coming out of Huntsville Alabama. The mystery slaughter of two men at the old Huntsville Airport was hot news for a while, but eventually, with no discernible progress made about the reason for the killings, and no perpetrator identified by the authorities, the story was soon replaced by the brutal murder of a young babysitter by a jealous wife, who suspected she was having an affair with her husband.

Sam got a call from Chief Alex Reagan to ask how his investigation was going. Sam said they were making slow progress, deciding it wouldn't be appropriate to reveal the details of their trip to Huntsville. Partially to save Reagan from being compromised, but there were also all manner of implications for him and Frankie if they admitted to shooting and killing three people, to say nothing of the unfortunate deaths of Larson Stipp and Abner Tuffin. Their two bodies had not yet been identified by the Huntsville cops. There would be little enough to work with from two such badly burnt corpses.

Sam told himself he would tell the captain the whole story later, but for now, he decided to keep it just between himself and Frankie.

"I assume you're going to still chase this thing down?" the captain asked.

"Yeah. Frankie and I are planning to fly up to Alabama again tomorrow, we're gonna pay a surprise visit to Gerald Jordan. We're going to follow the money. And there's certainly a lot of money sloshing around Sweet Clover Fields Farm."

"And how are you going to make Jordan talk to you?"

"We'll think of something."

The plane thumped down on to the runway at Atlanta airport at 11:14 a.m. Frankie and Sam deplaned and made their way to the car rental desks. It was raining as they drove away from the airport, but the clouds soon drifted away, and the day turned warm, sunny and dry.

Sweet Clover Farm looked the epitome of calm elegance. Sam got out and used the gate phone to gain entrance. Frankie looked on and realized Sam was having more of a prolonged conversation than seemed necessary. Sam put the phone back, walked to the car, and got it. The gate slowly opened.

"What was all that about?"

"Mr. Gerald Jordan himself answered the phone. I guess they have cameras watching the gate, so he knew it was us before I phoned. He refused to let us in, so I had to persuade him it was in his best interests to see us."

"And he agreed?"

"Sometimes you have to embroider things a little. I told him we had some very important information for him."

"Do we?"

"No, I lied. It's essential at times. It's a useful thing to remember in sleuthing."

"Every day I'm so grateful to you for imparting your invaluable wisdom to me." Sam laughed.

"Come on Frankie, cut the crap and let's go see the man."

"Yes, oh wise one, your wish is my command." Frankie put his foot down gently on the accelerator, and they moved slowly along the drive.

"But seriously, do we have any idea on what we're going to say? How we're going to approach this?"

"I just thought of a possible angle, so yes."

"Do I get to hear what it is?"

"Too late, I've not worked it out in full. Let's just wing it. Just follow my lead and feel free to join in 'cos I'll be making it all up as I go along."

"Oh right, that kind of plan," said Frankie, shaking his head and laughing. He parked the car, and they approached the door. The door opened before they could knock. Gerald Jordan stepped out, a shotgun hanging by his right-hand side.

"Okay, say what you got to say, then skedaddle."

"Now that's not the typical warm southern greeting we expected, is it Frankie?"

"Not even near. Anyone would think Mr. Jordan doesn't really like us."

"Oh, it's the comedy routine today is it, well I got better things to do than listen to you two clowns," Jordan raised his shotgun so it was pointing in the general area of their midriffs. "Git and git now."

"It was actually Mrs. Jordan, we came to see, not you, so maybe you could tell her we wish to speak with her." Just at that moment, Mary-Jo Jordan appeared by her husband's side.

"Now what on earth is going on Gerald? Why are you pointing that gun at these men? Put that gun down and invite them in. They've probably come a long way to see us, well me, if I heard the last part of the conversation correctly. Now do put that gun away Gerald. Come in, gentlemen." Gerald Jordan scowled, lowered his gun and moved to one side so they could pass. Sam looked at Frankie and shrugged, then Frankie followed Sam into the house, smiling at Gerald Jordan as he brushed past him.

They sat in the same cozy living room they'd sat in on the last occasion. Gerald came in and perched on the arm of a sofa, placing his shotgun, broken at the breech, across his knees. Sam and Frankie sat at opposite ends of the large sofa. The red setter got up from its place by the fireplace and came to sniff the new arrivals. Satisfied, it wandered back to the hearth rug, turned around twice, flopped down and fell asleep.

"Now what would you gentlemen like to drink, iced tea, lemonade, or something stronger maybe?" Sam and Frankie both asked for iced tea. "Would you mind telling Annie please Gerald?" Gerald looked discombobulated but shoved himself off the arm of the sofa and, with gun still in hand, went out of the room to give the order to Annie. Sam looked at Frankie both thinking the same thing. The dynamic between Mary-Jo and Gerald seemed to have dramatically changed, or maybe they just read it wrong the last time. Frankie also thought Mary-Jo herself had changed somehow. Despite her bossing Gerald around, she looked different, frail.

"Now I think I heard you say you wanted to speak with me."

Sam stood up and took out his phone, scrolled through it, went over to Mrs. Jordan and showed her the picture on the screen. She looked up at Sam.

"So, a picture of my boy Ricky," she said. "What do you want me to say?"

"Well, that's not Ricky Mrs. Jordan, that's a picture of Billy, Billy Fairman." She looked again, then her eyes misted over.

"My oh my," she said as if she'd entered a trance, I never could tell them apart." Sam looked across at Frankie.

"Never could tell who apart Mrs. Fairman?" Mary-Jo Jordan suddenly seemed to pull herself together.

"Sorry, who's this Billy, and why are you showing me this picture?" Gerald Jordan had walked back into the room.

"What's that you're showing my wife," he demanded and walked over to Sam. Sam turned the phone screen to Jordan's face.

"I'm showing her a picture of Billy Fairman, her son, brother of Richard, and one of the twins she bore and abandoned around January 1981." Mary-Jo Jordan looked at Gerald, who now looked as if he was about to self-combust.

"What's this shit you're peddling?"

"We have a DNA match to prove it," said Sam. Frankie looked down at the floor to conceal his own amazement at Sam's claim.

"No, you don't," said Gerald after recovering some of his composure. You can't have, it's not possible."

"Why, because you know the records on the blood sample taken when Ricky had his car crash were switched?"

"How...." Gerald Jordan ran out of words, then brought up his shotgun and pointed it at Sam. Sam was still standing by Mary-Jo's chair. "Go sit with your buddy on the sofa now! And keep your hands where I can see 'em." Annie knocked on the door as she entered the room with a tray. Gerald Jordan lowered his shotgun a little.

"Not now Annie," said Mrs. Jordan. Annie turned around and left the room, seemingly oblivious of the drama being acted out. Frankie was the first to speak.

"You're going to make one hell of a mess if you shoot us with that in your living room."

"Believe me, I will if necessary." Gerald Jordan replied.

"So, where do we go from here?" asked Sam. Mary-Jo stood up. Today's attire comprised a lilac blouse with ruffles at the neck, fancy leather belt holding up her pale blue jeans, tucked into thigh high shiny pale brown tooled leather cowboy boots with high Cuban heels and pointy toes. She looked stylish and younger than her years, but tired. She paced, looked at Gerald and then at Sam and Frankie.

"It's hard to explain without telling you the whole story."

"Mary-Jo, no," said Gerald Jordan

"I'm tired of all this... keeping secrets, living a lie. My son gunned down for what? And by whom?" She sat down, buried her head in her hands and sobbed quietly. Nobody moved. She recovered, blew her nose into a tissue, wiped the tears from her eyes, sat up and composed herself.

"Put that thing down Gerald," she said, Gerald obeyed. "Can you find out who killed my son, detective? I mean Billy, of course."

"Was that the name you gave him?" asked Sam

"It was," she said. "I called my twins William and Richard. Both names of the Kings of England." Sam nodded and continued.

"If we have enough information, I guess there's a good chance we can find out who killed Billy."

"Don't do this Mary-Jo," implored Gerald. She ignored his plea and told him to ask Annie to bring in the drinks again. Gerald scowled as he went out of the room. He came back in, followed by Annie, who served the drinks, then left. Mary-Jo took a sip of iced tea, then began her story.

"Before I begin, I want your solemn promise this will remain absolutely confidential. You must promise not to tell any other party. Do I have that promise"

"You do," said Frankie.

"Likewise," said Sam, "I promise." She looked at them both intently, first Sam, then at Frankie, then seemed to come to a decision.

"Okay. I was born in 1963. Unfortunately, my mother died giving birth. She had no relatives, so as I told you before, I was an orphan. My name was Mary-Jo Anderson back then. The first orphanage cared for me as a baby but then as I was moved to another one, things changed. I came to puberty when I was around ten or eleven years old, and then things that were, shall I say, out of the ordinary started to happen. I don't want to go into detail, I'm sure you can guess well enough the sort of abuse that went on in those days. I guess it still does. I resisted to begin with, and put up a fight, but I didn't stand a chance. I was punished harshly if I refused, and well rewarded if I complied. You soon learn."

"I became quite accomplished, and if I say so myself, I was quite beautiful back then. I became a favorite. I don't know how much the pervert pimps who ran the place were making, but I guess it was a lot. The 'clients,'" said Mary-Jo using air quotes, "were quite well-heeled businessmen in the main. Then one day, the day after my thirteenth birthday, I had a special visitor. I knew he was special because of all the fuss they made. I had to wear my best clothes, which is ironic when you think about it. This man was obviously very important, but he also wanted something that had never happened before. He wanted to film us doing it."

"I didn't know what to make of this, but I was promised a big bonus if I went along with it. I knew the unstated flip side of that would be severe punishment. And so, I performed, not just for Mr. Clarke, which was not his real name as I discovered later, but for the camera as well. I had to get used to there being a cameraman in the room, but like all things, I did get used to it in the end. In fact, I got a little friendly with the cameraman and had a couple of conversations with him in the minutes before my client came into the room. He showed me the little cartridges he used to record the film."

"One day the camera guy told me he wouldn't be coming back, that a new guy would be coming in his place. He never explained why or where he was going. But anyway, he gave me a cassette and told me to hide it. He said it might come in handy one day. I had no idea why he thought I would find the cassette useful. I didn't have anything to play it on. He didn't say if the film was of me and Mr. Clarke or something else altogether, but I assumed it was the former."

"Nevertheless, I did as he said and hid it in my special hiding place and forgot about it." Mary-Jo stopped talking and took another sip of her iced tea. Gerald was now slumped in his chair, a grim look on his face.

"So, after a while, two or three months maybe, Mr. Clarke told me he wouldn't be coming round to visit any more and gave me an envelope with some cash in it. He didn't explain why he wouldn't be visiting again. I thought maybe he was moving to another part of the country, or had simply got bored with me, I didn't find out till much later."

"At about the same time, we got a new warden. He was really mean and abusive. I'd been taken advantage of before, of course, but never had I met anyone as brutal as this guy. I was friends with another girl in the institution. Janice Hopkins. She was a little older than me, fifteen, I think. We decided to run away and made our plans to escape. Escaping wasn't difficult at all, but as we soon found out, surviving outside the institution was really hard. We had very little money, nowhere to stay and after the second night of sleeping rough, we were about to go back and ask to be allowed back into the institution when we met Gerald."

"Gerald is much older than me and, at the time, recently divorced. Janice and I moved into Gerald's trailer, but that didn't work out for long. Janice wanted to have Gerald for herself, but Gerald was only interested in me. We all had a huge fight one night, which resulted in Janice leaving. I never saw or heard from her again. Gerald and I became, what they call today, an item. The timing was unfortunate. The second week I was with Gerald, I discovered I was pregnant."

"I was scared, terrified that Gerald would kick me out, so I said nothing for a while. Eventually, I felt I had to tell Gerald. His first reaction was one of disbelief. He'd always used protection."

"Excuse me, Mrs. Jordan. But you said you were just fourteen?"

"Yes, I know what you're thinking. That Gerald was committing a crime by having sex with me. The thing is, I told him I was sixteen. I'd have told any lie to stop having to go back to that place. But fortunately, I did love Gerald, so in my mind, that made it all okay. Later, Gerald discovered I'd lied to him about my age, and he was a bit upset, but I told him he shouldn't feel guilty. That I'd misled him at the time for good reason."

"So, anyway, back to when I found out I was pregnant. I came clean and told him it could only be Mr. Clark's child. I expected him to kick me out, but," Mary-Jo looked over at Gerald and smiled a small smile, "Gerald didn't throw me out. He didn't ask me to have an abortion, either. It would have been a back street procedure in those days, and neither Gerald nor I wanted to take the risk. And you may think it surprising, but I'm also quite religious."

"So, one day when I was going through my things, the film cassette fell out of the bag I'd kept it in. Gerald was there and picked it up. He knew what it was, but not what was on it. He knew everything about my past, so I told him what I thought was probably on it."

"Gerald had a friend who was into photography, filming and stuff. He took it to him, and he asked if he could use his projector, or whatever it was, to see what was on the film. I was sure Gerald wouldn't want to watch the movie for titillation or perverse reasons. He just wasn't like that. Anyway, Gerald recognized the man in the film. The man who called himself Mr. Clarke had become a very powerful and influential politician, and I was pregnant with his child."

"Gerald was quite firm and said this man should be made to pay. I persuaded Gerald that I didn't want to go that route and he didn't push it any more at the time. I gave birth to twins. We couldn't afford to raise one child, let alone two. It became obvious that we needed to do something, so we tapped into a sort of unofficial network that placed unwanted babies with families desperate to adopt, but for various reasons couldn't do it through official channels. Nice people in the main just didn't pass the official sniff test. You get the picture."

"We came across this really nice lady who'd just lost both her husband and her baby in a car crash. It was a tragic situation, and she was desperate to adopt."

"A Mrs. Fairman by any chance?" asked Frankie

"Yes, Louise Fairman. We gave one of my twins to Louise. We agreed this arrangement would remain binding and absolutely secret.

But dark secrets have a habit of finding the light. I digress, back to my story. So, even with just the one child to look after, we were struggling. Gerald lost his job, I was looking after Ricky so I couldn't work. So, Gerald took it upon himself to get in touch with Mr. Clarke and ask for help. At least that's what he said he was going to do," Gerald Jordan spoke.

"Mary-Jo, enough, please stop. You don't know what you're doing, spilling the beans to these two…, these two goons." Mary-Jo stopped talking and took a long sip of her iced tea.

"No Gerald, we need to find out who killed my son. It's my duty as a mother. I will not see one of my children murdered and do nothing about it. Now where was I? Oh yes, so when I just said that Gerald asked for help from Mr. Clarke, that's a little disingenuous of me. I found out that Gerald not only asked for help but also told Mr. Clarke that we had him on tape or film or whatever it's called. And that a copy was lodged in a safe place and should anything untoward happen to either of us, then it would be released."

"What is Mr. Clarke's real name and just what is he now that makes him so powerful?" asked Sam. Mary-Jo looked at Gerald, who shook his head.

"I'm not prepared to say. As you might have guessed, the central part of the arrangement was that we would never reveal his real identity. And Lord only knows what he'd do if we broke our promise on that."

"I assume that your Mr. Clarke knew about the twins, their separation and adoption by Mrs. Fairman?"

"Yes, he did. We told him everything."

"And he never questioned if he was the father?"

"Yes, he did at first. So, he arranged for me to take Ricky to a doctor who took a blood sample from Ricky. Just to be sure he wouldn't cheat, we demanded a sample of Mr. Clarke's blood from the doctor conducting the test so we could do our own independent test if necessary. Although we knew he could have that fixed that with the doctor, but we thought we'd try, anyway.

"And the test confirmed he was the father?"

"I assume so. It was never mentioned again."

"Okay, we'll leave that for now, but I have to tell you Mrs. Jordan, that after I'd been to meet Louise Fairman, to ask her for information about Billy, to help in our investigation into his murder, someone arranged to have me kidnapped, drugged and interrogated. These same people, we assume, have has since sent people to try to kill me and Frankie here, on two occasions." Mary-Jo looked genuinely shocked.

"Who on earth would do that?"

"Your Mr. Clarke seems a prime candidate in the circumstances. But I can't figure out he how would have known about me going to see Mrs. Fairman? And why did an innocent visit prompt such a violent response? I can only assume he thought I knew more than I did. What's more, when I asked Mrs. Fairman if she could provide me with any useful information about Billy that would help us find his killer, she acted strange, as if she just wanted rid of me. Wouldn't answer any questions at all. Didn't seem interested in why her son was killed. So, I followed her to try to find out more."

"Maybe it was the following her that made them think I knew something. That's the only thing that makes sense, I guess."

"I'd already told Louise about Billy's death, even before the police went to tell her."

"When did you tell her?"

"The day it happened. Ricky called his dad and told him. Gerald naturally told me. And despite our agreement never to get in touch with one another, I felt obliged to tell Louise Fairman." Sam was silent for a few seconds.

"You haven't met with her since the handover, but you had her cellphone number?"

"No, of course not. I had her original landline number. She's old-fashioned like me, and she'd kept it. Do think I'd lie to you about this, now I've bared my soul to you?"

"No, I don't, I apologize," said Sam.

"I should think so detective."

"But why didn't Mrs. Fairman want to answer any questions about Billy?" Sam asked.

"I can only guess she thought that if anyone started digging around, it might be found she adopted Billy unofficially, probably illegally. If that came to light, it might mean trouble for both her and me. Although why anyone would care after all this time.... Anyway, maybe she also knew that whatever she told you, it wouldn't bring Billy back."

"I guess you're right. I suppose she thought the whole thing might start to unravel," said Sam, nodding to himself.

"Please carry on with your story, Mrs. Jordan," said Frankie, not wanting to lose the momentum.

"Well, Mr. Clarke wasn't prepared to get directly involved in helping us but used his connections and knowledge to help us out, well help me out really. Gerald acted as go between. After a week or so after we'd first contacted him, Clarke told us he knew of a farm. It was this one, which at the time was really run down, a wreck of a place."

"The farm had an extremely poor record of providing a living for the people who worked it. The owner had recently died, and it was put up for sale by his three children. They'd fled years before to seek a better life elsewhere. After the death of their father, their mother left to go and live with one of them."

"Due to his position, Clarke told us he had privileged knowledge about reserves of fossil fuels in various areas in the state. Apparently, he was aware there were almost certainly modest reserves of oil underneath this property. And so he told us, well that is, he told me, to buy the farm. We told him we had no money, but he said I should apply for a loan from a particular bank. That the loan would be granted without fuss."

"Surely he'd be in big trouble if stuff like that ever got out, abusing his position, as whatever it is he is, to do someone a favor?"

"It was only ever in conversations over the phone. He never identified himself in those conversations. And it wasn't like today where everyone has a phone they can record conversations on. Anyway, we already had more than enough to ruin him. And why would we expose him and deprive ourselves of a decent life? No detective, mutual interest ensured his secrets were safe enough with us."

"And the rest, as they say, is history, and much as we told you previously. The only thing was, the yield of oil was far more than Clarke or whoever's expert opinion he'd listened to, had expected." Mary-Jo stopped talking briefly. "I think that's enough for now, I'm tired."

"We do have some questions, Mrs. Jordan," said Frankie. "For instance, was Ricky aware he had a twin brother?"

"No, and I don't know how he would have found out." Sam jumped in

"Do you have any idea who might want to harm or kill Billy?"

"No, no idea whatsoever."

"You?" said Sam, looking over at Gerald.

"No, I don't. But I have a question for you."

"Okay."

"How d'you know about the DNA samples being switched?"

"I didn't. I didn't even know I was going to say it until I walked in the room earlier. Call it an inspired guess." Jordan nodded his head and grimaced.

"I shoulda known."

"I'm exhausted. I'm going for a rest," said Mary-Jo. If you want any more information, you can call me tomorrow. You have my number. Good day gentlemen." And with that she got up and walked out of the door.

"We'll see ourselves out," said Frankie. Gerald Jordan remained where he was, a thoughtful frown on his face.

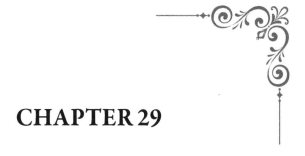

CHAPTER 29

They got back into the rental car. Frankie drove through the gate, along the road, found a place to park, and switched off the engine.

"Wow," he said, rubbing his forehead, "Mary-Jo's little monologue back there raises more questions than it answers."

"It sure does, partner. Did you think she looked a bit, I don't know, unwell, or was it my imagination?"

"Now you mention it, I think she did. But I think telling us that story was emotionally draining. Re-living her time as an orphan and what that man did to her. Not many people could survive all that and stay normal."

"I guess you're right."

"By the way, that stunt about knowing they'd switched the DNA. That was inspired."

"It worked, thank God,"

"It did, but how would they have done it?"

"The usual, money. Find out someone with access to the evidence records and come up with a big enough bribe...."

"Yes, but how could they be switched?"

"Swap the sample for someone else's, would be the simplest method. Money will find a way. Now, we need answers to these other questions." Sam used his fingers to emphasize the point. "One, who is Mr. Clarke and what is he now? Two, Gerald was divorced, so who was his first wife, and did he have any children by her? And Three, is Clarke involved with the rogue Feds who tried to kill us? If so, is he in cahoots with Gerald and to what end? And that's only for starters."

"And - would Mr. Clarke be involved in killing one of his own kids?"

"That's a very good point. One thing we do know is that someone involved in that film crew was feeding information back to whoever was trying to kill us." Sam said, "so who is that person?"

"Maybe look at why they, whoever 'they' are, why they wanted, or maybe still want to kill us. The mysterious Mr. Clarke obviously wants to keep the lid on his past sexual peccadillos. Having sex and filming himself having sex with a minor would be pretty devastating for anyone, especially a politician. Apart from a fall from grace, he'd be facing jail time, wouldn't he Sam?"

"Well, there were some pretty strange laws in some states back then, age of consent and marriage and such. But, yeah, I reckon a sex tape involving a minor, a child really, would be dynamite for anyone and especially for a prominent political figure. But that aside for a minute, we're still no nearer knowing who killed Billy Fairman and why he was killed. We've got a whole load of information now, information overload really, but we still haven't established a motive for the murder."

"So, how do we proceed?"

"Follow the money Frankie, follow the money. I suspect Gerald could be the key to this. He probably knows a lot more than he's saying. But how do we get him to talk?"

CHAPTER 30

Sam and Frankie flew back to Fort Myers, arriving late evening, and collected Frankie's jeep from the parking lot. It was a forty-five minute drive to Naples along the I-75, depending on traffic. They drove in silence for a while, each lost in their own thoughts.

"Been a long day, there's lots to think about."

"There sure is Frankie, there sure is."

"Well, it's your show, so what's our next move?"

"I say we don't try to analyze anything just now. My brain's hurting, I just want to get home, kiss my wife, take a hot shower, have a beer, a bite to eat, and a long sleep. I find sleep helps my mind process stuff like this, most times better than when I'm awake."

"I know what you mean Sam. I think we should maybe go see Ricky and Clive and the film crew tomorrow, but how much do we tell 'em?"

"I'm still thinking on that. But before we do that, we need to go see Captain Alex Reagan, lay it all out for him. He's got the resources to find out stuff we can't, so..."

"Yes, good call. Ah, here we go, Pine Ridge Road coming up."

They turned off the highway. Frankie drove to Sam's house, dropped him off, then called Daisy to see if she was still up and maybe interested in a late supper at his place. He was wired and needed a drink and some distraction. She could also bring his little dog Charlie back with her.

Sam collected Frankie the next morning, and they drove to Naples Police Headquarters, arriving at 1030, as arranged earlier, with Captain Reagan. Reagan's assistant showed them into his office and closed the door. The captain was busy on a call but motioned them to sit. He finished his call.

"Good morning, Sam, Frankie. I think we should really have Dale at this meeting. He is, after all, the official police detective investigating this case." He saw the look on Sam's face. "I know that look, so what's the problem Sam?"

"Well sir, a few lines may have been crossed, and I'd really like to tell you our story off the record first, as it were. There's also a.., a caveat."

"Oh," said Reagan, "Hmm..." He scribbled on his yellow pad, tore off the page and pushed it over to Sam. Malfeasance involved? Sam scribbled yes maybe and shoved it back. The captain looked at it, stood up, and put the piece of paper in his pocket. "Look, it's a nice sunny day and I've been cooped up in this office since 7:00 a.m. I need to stretch my legs. You okay if we go out for a little stroll?"

"Sure," said Sam. Frankie nodded, and they got up and followed the captain out of the station. There was a small park across the road featuring an ornamental lake, populated mainly by ducks. A few minutes later, they were sitting on a bench by the lake.

"Okay, let's have it," said the captain. Sam took a deep breath and began.

"Well, first the caveat. We gave our solemn promise not to tell part of the story to any third party, so we have a dilemma. We really need to tell you everything, but you have to agree to be bound by the same promise."

"That's a big ask Sam."

"I know, but you've known me for a long time captain and vice versa, and you know I wouldn't ask this if it wasn't absolutely necessary." Reagan stroked his chin. Sam continued, "then we'll trust you to make a judgment about what should be left in or taken out, for the formal report, that is. And before Dale's invited into this?"

"Hmm, not sure I like the sound of all this at all, but go ahead. I'll keep your promise if that's what it takes. Do you want me to spit on my hands and shake?" said the captain, feigning sincerity. Sam smiled.

"I don't think that will be necessary."

"Okay, shoot." Sam and Frankie told Reagan everything, leaving nothing out. Reagan stopped them to clarify details of the drone attack, then told them to carry on. He interrupted just once more when Sam told him about Bentley's attempt to shoot them and how Frankie had no choice but to respond in kind. He asked a couple of questions to clarify the sequence of events, but then left them to tell the rest of their story in their own way. When they'd finished, he looked grim, stroked his chin again and said nothing for a while, then spoke.

"Okay. First, thank you for being frank, excuse the pun," he said, looking at Frankie, "I don't need to tell you, that it could get very messy if this went up the line. So, in the interests of saving a lot of police time in futile investigations into the minutia of why what and how, and the mountain of paperwork it would generate, I'm going to suggest we write up a slightly er..., shall we say, sanitized version of events as an interim report. You're experienced enough a police detective to know what to do Sam, so let's just leave it at that. Let me have it as soon as possible. Like I said, I really should invite Dale Vogel into this, but under the circumstances, I think it wise to leave this with you two, at least for now."

"And, it goes without saying, I think we all need to be very careful with this one. Anything that involves a supposedly powerful political figure is a potential can of worms. We're going to have to tread very carefully and keep all this confidential and between us three for the time being. I'm happy for you to use resources in my department to get any additional information you can't get any other way. And I know I don't really have to say this, but I will. Any other parties who need to be involved only need to be told the minimum to obtain anything you're trying to find out about anything or anyone."

"Not sure we'd find anything about this orphanage in Mapletown, Safe Harbor, was it?" Sam nodded. "A lot of those places were closed down, so the chances are we'd find nothing, no records. Anything specific I can help with at the moment?"

"Yes," Frankie said, "we could do with getting some background on Gerald Jordan. Where he was born, marriages, children, any convictions, any links or connection to the Feds. Anything at all, really."

"Okay, we can do that," said Reagan, taking out a small notebook and pen. Give me his details." Frankie gave him all they knew about Gerald Jordan and the address of Sweet Clover Farm. "Anything else?"

"Well, there's Mr. Bentley deceased, aka James Royce, or the other way round," said Sam. We can give you the credentials we found on him. The office he used was short-term rental, so that's probably a dead end. Maybe worth looking into his background, although I'm not sure how that would help anything."

"I agree, "said Reagan, "looking into Royce's background won't achieve anything, and it might alert someone to connect his demise with this investigation, so we won't go there, ditto the two guys who died in the office in Huntsville and the two unfortunates in the truck. Let's just draw a veil over all that. No good will come from pursuing that line of enquiry. Out of self-interest, the Feds will probably wipe out any records of Royce's existence and that of the other operatives involved. So, is that it?"

"For the moment Cap," said Sam standing, Frankie followed suit, "We'll obviously keep you informed of any more progress we make, but that information on Gerald Jordan would be extremely useful."

"I'll get someone on to it as soon as I get back to the office. You should have it later today. What are your next moves?"

"We're going to call Mary-Jo Jordan back, ask her a couple of more questions, then go talk to the film crew, and Ricky Jordan and if he's around, and his manager and producer Ross Sharkey. See if we can get a bit more information on everyone's movements that day. I know Dale Vogel probably covered that ground, but we'd like to go over it with them again, see if there are any inconsistencies, etc."

"Okay, but careful you don't make Dale look a fool. I've got a police department to run here, and I don't want anyone walking round the place with wounded pride and a grudge and thinking they've been sidelined because of me."

"Understood Alex." They shook hands with the captain, and he left to walk back to the Naples Police Department.

They drove back to Frankie's condo to make the call to Mrs. Jordan. Frankie made more coffee and sitting at his dining table, they discussed what they wanted to ask.

"You think she'd answer any questions about her health?"

"Don't know, but let's put that on the list. We need to ask her about Gerald's first marriage. See what she knows about that."

"Okay, so who's going to talk to her?"

"Not sure she likes either of us more than the other, so?" Frankie took a coin out of his pocket, flipped it and caught it, covering his hand.

"Call."

"Heads," said Sam.

"Heads it is." Sam took out his cell and punched in the number. A woman answered, but it wasn't Mary-Jo.

"Jordan residence," the voice said.

"Annie?"

"Yes, Annie replied.

"This is Detective Randazzo, Sam Randazzo. My partner and I came to see Mrs. Jordan yesterday."

"Yes, I remember."

"May I speak with Mrs. Jordan please?"

"Well, I don't know, she's resting at the moment."

"Well, she did say to call her if we needed more information."

"I'll go see, please wait." Sam looked at Frankie. "She's resting." Frankie nodded. Sam switched his attention back to his cell.

"Yes Mrs. Jordan, sorry to disturb you, and thanks for taking my call. I just have two or three questions if you can help me out. I'll try to keep it brief."

"Okay detective, ask away." She sounded weary.

"Did Gerald have any children from his first marriage?"

"He had a child, I think, but he doesn't like to talk about his first marriage. It was a bit of a disaster from the little I know. He said he had no contact with the child since they split. The mother, his wife, moved far away. I stopped asking him about it because it caused him so much stress. He said it was a part of his life that he'd wiped from his memory. I saw little point in pursuing the subject. None of my business, really."

"Okay, thanks. Next, yesterday you corrected yourself when you said Clarke told us to buy the farm, then you said he told me to buy the farm. I checked with public records this morning and it seems the farm is your name only."

"Yes it is, Mr. Clarke insisted on it."

"How does that sit with Gerald?"

"Gerald is well looked after. He gets a generous income for life from the proceeds of the oil sales. More than enough, I can assure you, detective. Certainly over $200, 000 a year."

"I don't doubt your generosity, Mrs. Jordan."

"Thank you, detective, anything else?"

"Well, you may think my next question impudent and insensitive, so I apologize in advance if you do, but I have to ask it. If you pass before your husband, does he get ownership of the farm?" There was a silence. Same waited. "Mrs. Jordan, are you still there?"

"Yes. I'm still trying to make my mind up whether to provide an answer."

"All I can say, Mrs. Jordan, is that my motive for asking is to gather as much information I can in order to catch the killer of your son Billy. I have no other motive for asking."

"That's a very persuasive argument, detective. Okay, no, Gerald doesn't inherit the farm. On my death, my lawyers are instructed to sell the farm, divide the proceeds and give half to Billy Fairman anonymously. That is obviously not going to be that the case now, so I have to alter my will accordingly. But the agreement regarding Gerald remains in place until his demise. Any new owner would have to abide by that agreement"

"Does Gerald know the details of your will?"

"No, nobody else knows, not Gerald, Not Louise Fairman, nobody. That's strictly confidential between myself and my lawyer. Like I say, Gerald knows that his own agreement will continue after my death. I'm sure he just assumes the farm will go to Ricky."

"And do I assume that neither Ricky nor Billy Fairman were aware they'd be sharing the inheritance?"

"No, definitely not. Neither of them knows, or should I say knew. I'm sure Ricky also assumed he would be left everything, and now he will. But there was more than enough to go round, so in the event that Billy hadn't met such an untimely death, I don't think only getting half would have been a problem for Ricky.

"I wanted to do right by them both, even if it was after I'd passed on. I'm a southern gal and despite my actions as a young girl, I still believe in the Almighty, redemption and honesty and basic decency."

"I get it Mrs Jordan And thank you for answering my questions, I hope I didn't distress you too much."

"No, you didn't, detective. I want my son's killer caught, so offending my sensitivities is a small price to pay if it helps you get a result. I am also going to answer a question you didn't ask. It can't have escaped your attention that I am not in the best of health. I won't say more, but Gerald is almost certain to survive me. Now I hope there are no more questions, detective. I bid you goodbye."

"Goodbye Mrs. Jordan," Sam said, but she'd already gone.

"From the look on your face, that was a worthwhile conversation." Sam repeated the conversation to Frankie.

"Wow," was all Frankie could say when Sam had finished. "There's a motive in their somewhere, but how does killing Billy achieve anything for anyone?"

"It doesn't, not on the face of it."

"Come on, let's go talk to Clive and the film crew and Ricky Jordan, see what gives," said Frankie.

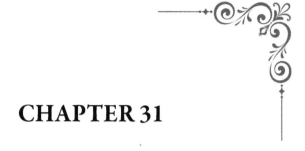

CHAPTER 31

As arranged earlier in the morning, Frankie picked Sam up at his home. Sam walked down his garden path, turned and waved goodbye to his wife Martha and got in the jeep.

"Where are we heading?"

"I called Clive Susman earlier and asked to see him. He's still working at the shop in the mall, so he suggested we meet him there."

"The scene of the crime. Is that significant?"

"No, I don't think so. They're pulling out of here in the next day or so, so they're sorting through what they take and what they leave, plus he says, they're using it to plan the next schedule of shots and catch up on editing and stuff." They got to Third, parked and got out of the car to cross the road to the abandoned shopping mall.

Third street was busy as usual. Waiters bussing tables in anticipation of the lunchtime crowd. Early morning tourists checking out the shops and restaurant menus, or just having a coffee in one of the many outdoor cafes. Frankie never tired of Third with its gentle bustle, floral decorations, colorful shops and the inevitable super cars parked up attracting admiring glances. Music emanated from the talented street buskers entertaining passersby.

A motorist stopped to let them cross the road and soon they were knocking on the door of the very same shop where they'd found the body of Billy Fairman. Clive opened the door and waved them in.

"Hi guys, help yourself to coffee. It's over there. Excuse me while I just finish off on this schedule." Frankie wandered over to where a coffee pot sat on a Mr. Coffee machine and poured himself a cup. He looked at Sam.

"Not for me, thanks," he said, wandering through to the rear of the shop. He came into the back, to where Clive was. "You here on your own today Clive?"

"Yeah, the others are out, just filming a few short clips we need for editing purposes." He counted down a list he'd made and put the clipboard down. "Okay, that's finished. Now, what can I do for you two gentlemen?"

"Just tying up some loose ends Clive. On the day Billy was killed, you'd arranged to meet him here at what, 11:00 a.m.?"

"Yes, I think so. Originally, I think it was 10:00 a.m. but if you remember, I called you to say we were running late, as usual, and changed it to 11:00 a.m. I think.

"So, did you all make your own way to this place that morning, or had you all met up before and traveled here in one group?"

"No, we all traveled separately I think, and arranged to meet up initially at Bad Ass Coffee, that little place around the corner. Parking's easier there. Then we all walked round here, and we met you."

"So, just to be sure, everyone traveled separately to Bad Ass Coffee that morning?"

"Well, I'm not exactly sure. Some of them could have come together. I wasn't really taking that much notice. As long as they all turned up, it didn't matter. Seems Billy didn't get told we were running late, so I guess he went to the shop early. He had a key. Maybe some of the others traveled together, I don't know. I'd met with Ricky at 8:30 that morning to go through a few things and we traveled down here together in my car."

"Okay, so that's different to what you said before, when you said everyone traveled separately, I mean."

"Yes, I'm sorry, I didn't know you wanted me to be so precise. Is there a point to these questions, Sam?"

"It's just a question of alibis, that's all," Susman looked horrified

"Alibis, are you kidding me?" You suspect the killer is one of our people who came along to the meeting that morning?"

"Well, someone shot and killed Billy Fairman, didn't they?"

"Yes, but...."

"Look Clive, we're just doing our job. So, you're saying that you and Ricky can provide an alibi for each other? Were you together the whole time from 08:30 until you arrived here?"

"Yes, but why do you think either Ricky or I would need an alibi? This is crazy."

"Crazy or not," said Sam, "alibis help. We need to talk to all the others who were here that morning. When will they be back?" Clive looked as if he was about to lose his cool, Frankie thought, but then seemed to relax. He picked up his clipboard again.

"In a couple of hours, I guess. I can call you when they return. But Ross won't be with them, she's gone away for a couple of days on business."

"Okay Clive, call me when you know what time they'll be back here. See you later."

"Yeah, see you later," said Clive.

"Where to now Sam?"

"Let's go to that Bad Ass Coffee place."

They walked around down third across 13th on to the coffee shop. They went in, ordered their drinks, then went to sit outside.

"Good coffee," said Frankie, taking a sip. "Clive seem a bit jumpy to you? I mean, when you mentioned alibis and all that."

"He didn't like the implication for sure. There's something we're missing." Frankie took another sip of his drink, "The problem for me is motive. We followed the money, and it led us to the Sweet Clover Fields Farm."

"Mary-Jo's leaving the farm to Ricky, and I can see why that would make Gerald a bit miffed. Or maybe not. I mean, his son gets to own the farm, well stepson. And as I understood it, the agreement to pay Gerald a handsome income continues after she passes. Why would anyone be unhappy with a deal like that?"

"You're right Frankie. Who would benefit from the death of Billy Fairman, other than Ricky Jordan? But Mary-Jo swears Ricky doesn't know Billy would inherit half her estate, and neither does Gerald. And would Ricky really kill Billy so he could get his hands on the entire estate instead of half? Like Mary-Jo says, there's more than enough to go round, so would he take the risk?"

"Greed is a powerful emotion in some people Sam."

"I suppose so, even so, I can't quite see it. And, of course, we could be barking up the wrong tree altogether. His killing could be for another reason, entirely unrelated to his family. Could be a crime of passion, a jealous husband. Maybe he'd got into debt, or gambled, borrowed money and stiffed someone. Or maybe it was drug related. I don't know. I'm having another coffee, you?"

"Yeah, why not? We have time to kill." Just as Sam stood up, his cell rang. He sat down again and answered. "Yes Alex." He listened for a while, then said, "Well, I'll be damned. Yeah, thanks, very interesting." Sam put his cell down on the table.

"Come on," said Frankie, "give."

"Right, well, that was Captain Reagan. He had someone look into Gerald Jordan's past. Jordan had a son with his first wife. They divorced some years before he met Mary-Jo."

"Okay, and..."

"You won't believe this."

"Try me."

"His wife's maiden name was Susman."

"Holy moley!"

"Did you really just say holey moley?"

"I'm ashamed to say I did." Sam shook his head.

"Hmm, so do we now know who was probably passing information back from the film set? If so, it implicates Clive as being in league with whoever was trying to kill us."

"Seems a distinct possibility. Perhaps more than a possibility Frankie, but why?"

"Well, the links are obvious, Clive to Gerald and Gerald to Mr. Clarke. Mr. Clarke, we're told, is powerful, paranoid and ruthless. And, as we know, only too willing to go to any lengths to eliminate any potential threat to his standing and political career."

"Yeah, you're right Frankie. And he must also know if his past caught up with him, he could be ruined, maybe even be facing jail time. In my experience, there will likely be other victims Clarke abused. And if it was proved he filmed himself having sex with a minor and it got into the public domain, he'd be in big trouble. Maybe other victims would come forward?"

"If you're right and Gerald lets Mr. Clarke know that Mary-Jo's told us the whole story, he'll be even more determined to eliminate us as a threat, won't he?"

"He will, for sure. And, important as that is, put it to one side for a minute and consider this. We're still no nearer to finding out why Billy Fairman was killed, and who killed him, are we?

"But we now know a man who might help us find out. Let's go." They got up and walked back along Third, back up the steps to the mall, knocked on the shop door and entered. Clive was on his cell phone. He looked flustered when he saw them walk in.

"I'll call you back," he said to whoever was on the other end, then continued. "Yes, it's the two detectives, they're back. Okay. Yes, I understand." He put his cell in his pocket. "The others aren't back yet," he said, walking over to the door, opening it and looking out, scanning the mall before closing it again.

"Actually, it was you we wanted to talk to," said Frankie.

"Oh," said Clive, looking less than happy.

"You haven't been straight with us Clive, have you?" Frankie continued, "By the way, you do know Florida still has the death penalty for murder one, don't you?" Clive was now looking decidedly jumpy. He hesitated, then reached around his back, pulled out a gun, and said,

"Don't," as both Sam and Frankie instinctively reached for theirs. "Take out your guns with your thumb and finger, place them on the floor, then kick them over to me. It's a cliché I know, but one wrong move and I'll shoot to kill. And I know how to use this, believe me."

They complied. Susman kicked the guns to the side of the room.

"How did you know?"

"We didn't. We had our suspicions, but you've just helped confirm them Clive, so thanks for that."

"Fuck you," he replied and just so you know, I'm just as good a shot with either hand, so, if you want to live...." Clive left the sentence unfinished and transferred his gun to his left hand.

"You're not going to get away with this Clive," said Frankie, "The Naples police know where we are, and they know about you and who your father is. You're done, Clive, well and truly finished."

"Just shut the fuck up or I'll kill you here and now, you hear me?" Clive's voice had gone up an octave and Frankie thought he sounded on the verge of hysteria. Clive continued, "Now, each of you, lace your fingers together and put your hands behind your head. Now!" Sam and Frankie both raised their arms and laced their hands behind their heads. Clive gave a little laugh.

"Done this scene so many times making movies. Great practice for the real thing." He's manic, thought Sam. Clive continued, "okay now turn around and walk slowly into the back room. No funny stuff now, just walk nice and slow." Clive walked behind them, keeping his distance.

"Okay stop," Clive moved round to the side nearest Frankie. "Okay, now kneel. Sam kneeled down, one knee first, then the other. "You too Frankie, come on, chop chop." Frankie kneeled down. Clive dug into his pocket with his right hand, and took out his cellphone, all the time looking at Frankie and Sam. Clive looked down at his phone briefly, thumb ready to press to make a call. The distraction was enough for Frankie. He fell sideways off his knees, executing a scissor kick and taking Susman's legs from underneath him. Clive crashed to the ground, his gun and phone skittering across the polished wooden floor. Clive reached out for his gun. Quick as a flash, Sam jumped up and stamped hard on Susman's outstretched arm. The noise of bone breaking was audible. Clive Susman screamed in agony, then fainted.

"Nice move, Sam," said Frankie, getting up off the floor.

"Nice move yourself, Frankie." Sam stood over Susman. As he did so, the pain woke Clive Susman up. Sam put his foot down firmly on the damaged arm. Clive howled in agony again, then closed his eyes and lay back on the floor, whimpering. Sam took his foot away.

"Just making sure," he said, smiling.

"I'll get our guns," said Frankie and went to the front of the shop. Sam picked up Clive's gun and cellphone, unloaded the gun and put them all in his pockets.

Frankie came back and gave Sam his gun back.

"I'm going to call Captain Reagan. We need this guy arrested and get him some medical treatment, then we need to decide our next move." Sam made the call end explained the situation. Two uniforms arrived at the shop at the same time as the film crew. Shortly afterwards, a klaxon announced the arrival of an ambulance and paramedics.

Sam stayed in the shop to deal with the cops arresting Susman. Frankie took charge of the film crew and asked the head cameraman, Doug Ramsay, to move his men away from the immediate area of the shop. They stood in a small group in the mall, obviously curious and confused. Satisfied Sam didn't need him further, Frankie went over to the crew and told them there'd been a problem and Clive had sustained a minor injury.

"I thought Ricky would be coming with you," Frankie said

"He was going to come along, but he got a call just as we'd finished the last session and said he had to leave urgently," said Doug, shrugging his shoulders.

"You know who the call was from?"

"No, but it looked kinda serious. We'd all been laughing and joking, but after Ricky got that call, I guess you'd say he looked a might grim. So, what kind of trouble is Clive in? Cops and medics - don't look good."

"'Sorry to sound mysterious, but I'm afraid I can't say at the moment Doug."

"Well, we've finished the last few bits and pieces now, so it was going to be an editing session tomorrow, but don't look like Clive will be available. Any idea when he'll be back?"

"Give me your cell number and I'll call you as soon as I know more, okay?"

Doug gave his number to Frankie. Doug then told the rest of the crew that business was over for the day, and they all left the mall. Sam strolled over to Frankie.

"Captain says need to go down the station and meet with him."

"Okay, let's go."

CHAPTER 32

They were shown straight into Captain Reagan's office.
"Take a seat, fellers. Tell me the story." So, they did. "Okay, well, your guy's all lawyered up now, so he's saying nothing other than he felt threatened by you two, so whatever he did, he acted in self-defense. Says you tried to pull a gun on him and he beat you to it. Says he disarmed you and was about to call the cops when you both assaulted him and broke his arm."

"That's simply not true, of course," said Frankie

"Yeah, but it's your word against his, no independent witness, so he's going to skate. I doubt we can hold him for long. They'll have him out of here by tomorrow at the latest, probably in a couple of hours, unless we get something more solid to charge him with. You got any plans to move this forward, Sam?"

"Yeah, Frankie and I discussed it in the car coming here. We're going to call Louise Fairman and go see Mary-Jo Jordan again, or more to the point, her husband Gerald."

"Okay. By the way, who's paying for all these trips?"

"The movie producer and Ricky Jordan's personal manager, Ross Sharkey. She hired us right after we discovered Billy's body."

"She know about this latest development?"

"Not yet, we're due to check in with her, but she moves around a lot. Oh, nearly forgot, here's Clive's cell and the handgun we took off him," said Sam, placing them both on Reagan's desk. "Doug, the head cameraman, told Frankie here that Ricky was with them and on the way to the shop just before we got into it with Clive. Says Ricky got a call and seemed spooked by it. He bailed, said he wasn't going to go with them to the meeting with Clive. Said he had somewhere else he had to be."

"And, that gun we took off Clive," said Sam, gesturing towards the black and silver gun on the desktop, "is a Smith and Wesson nine-millimeter. I took the bullets out already. The gun will have my prints on it and Frankie's, and Clive's, of course. But that obviously wasn't the gun that was used to kill Billy, being the wrong caliber an all."

"We'll check it out anyway, make sure it's legal and so on. Okay. Right, well, anything more you two need from me?"

"Yeah, there is," said Sam. "You remember, you got someone to check out that blood sample taken from Ricky Jordan when he was arrested for DUI, and checked it against Billy Fairman's DNA?"

"I do, why?"

"They didn't match, did they?"

"If you say so. I wasn't taking that much notice at the time," said Reagan. Sam gave the captain a moment to think it through. "Ah, I get it. Now the mother's confirmed they were identical twins, the DNA should have been a perfect match."

"Do identical twins always have the same DNA?" asked Frankie.

"Yes, they do," said Sam, "however...." Sam smiled and waited. The captain thought for a moment, then said,

"Uh hu, I get where you're going with this, the fingerprints?" Sam nodded. "You want me to pull the fingerprints from the DUI record?" Sam nodded again.

"Hang on," said Frankie, "DNA is always exactly the same, but identical twins have different fingerprints?" Sam smiled and nodded. "So," Frankie continued as if talking to himself, "we know the DNA should have been an exact match, because we now know Billy and Ricky were identical twins, but if Ricky Jordan's fingerprints on the DUI record, assuming they weren't switched as well, are a match to the fingerprints the ME took off the body we found, then it was Ricky Jordan who was killed in the shop. And the guy now acting as Ricky Jordan, isn't Ricky Jordan, and has to be... Billy Fairman. Wow!"

"Yep," said Sam, "we need to compare the finger prints of the body we found to the prints taken from the DUI record, see if they're a match or not."

"When did you figure that out?"

"Just now, as we walked into the Cap's office. The penny dropped. There's been something nagging me on the edge of my brain, and I couldn't quite get what it was until just now. See, I've been trying to figure the angle. What would be the benefit of Billy's death to any of the people involved? But if Ricky were to die, and Billy took his place, then Billy would inherit the lot when Mary-Jo passes, which sadly may not be all that far off."

"So, Clive, Gerald and Billy cooked up a deal which required them to kill Ricky Jordan so they could get their hands on the property, oil rights and everything, then share it out between all three of them."

"Yep, that's my guess. All we got to do now is prove it."

"I think you two are getting ahead of yourselves," Captain Reagan said, "it's pure speculation, at least until we get those fingerprint records. And even then, as Frankie here says, maybe they were switched as well."

"And how long is that going to take?"

"I guess I can apply some pressure and maybe call in a favor. But the truth is, I don't know."

"Okay Captain, Frankie and I will call it a day." Frankie dropped Sam off at his home then went to Naples pier to watch the fishermen and clear his head. The day was warm with a light breeze. He parked up on Thirteenth Avenue, strolled to the pier, then walked to the end where the more serious anglers tended to congregate.

Watching the men and women fishing was therapeutic. As he relaxed, he realized how tense he'd been feeling. Things could have gone south if Clive had been a bit more cautious about the way he'd handled them. That he got the drop on the two of them in the first place was a lesson never to take anything or anyone for granted. He took out his cell and called Daisy to see if she was free for dinner. He needed her company and a change of subject. She answered on the third ring.

"Hello stranger. I thought you'd maybe run off with some floozie. Then I thought, no, surely there aren't any women that desperate."

"You looking for trouble, lady?"

"No, I was looking for a good time. Are you going to wine and dine me and maybe take advantage of me when I'm tiddly?"

"Just give me half a chance, shweetheart."

"Was that Cary Grant?"

"Now you are looking for trouble. Be round at mine at seven and don't be late, understand?"

"Yes sir," she said laughing, and rang off. He got up and remembered Charlie hadn't had a walk since the morning.

CHAPTER 33

The day dawned brightly, with a few wispy clouds drifting along the horizon. Frankie woke up. His back still pained him and he had a bit of a headache from the night before. One martini too many, but he had no regrets. He and Daisy had hardly stopped laughing. He was grateful she hadn't asked him for any more details about his current case, probably sensed I needed a break from it thought Frankie, as he did his stretching exercises on the lanai.

Shortly afterwards, he took Charlie for his walk come run. As he jogged around Venetian Bay, he greeted the other early morning walker and runners.

After he'd finished his breakfast, he called Doug Ramsay. Doug answered on the first ring.

"Who is it?" Doug Ramsay asked.

"Frankie Armstrong. I'm calling to see if you've heard from Ricky."

"No, I haven't. He's not answering his cell, and neither is Clive. What the heck is going on Frankie? Where's Clive?"

"Clive's was detained. He pulled a gun on us yesterday."

"What?"

"'Fraid so Doug. Look, best you all take a couple of days off. Go to the beach or something, just till things calm down and get a bit clearer. I promise to let you know what's happening as soon as I know, okay?"

Frankie broke the connection before Doug could ask any more questions. A few minutes later, Sam called.

"Morning Sam."

"Hi Frankie. I called Ross Sharkey last night gave her a brief update. I didn't go into too much detail. Told her we wanted to check some things out before coming to any conclusions."

"She say anything helpful?"

"She seemed shocked, naturally. Couldn't believe it at first, but then said she'd had a strange feeling about the killing from the get go. Nothing made any sense, and she couldn't imagine why anyone would want to kill Billy Fairman. But nothing much more than that."

"She asked why I thought Clive had pulled a gun on us, but I thought it best to keep our suspicions to ourselves for the moment, so I acted dumb....don't!" Frankie laughed. "Then she told me to get on with it, spare no expense in bringing this thing to a conclusion. I'm torn Frankie. Do we go and see Gerald Jordan before we get the fingerprints, or do we have to wait?"

"The more I think about it, the more I think there's no other logical explanation. And where's Billy or Ricky or whoever he is? I called Doug Ramsay just now, and he hasn't heard from Ricky and says he's not answering his phone."

"Okay, I say we call Louise Fairman, see if Billy's been in touch with her. Then let's pay another visit to Mr. and Mrs. Jordan. I don't want to call ahead, we need to see them unannounced. Better that way, surprise visit, gauge their reactions."

"They might not be there."

"Where else would they be? They can't just lock that place up and go on vacation, can they? Anyway, we know Mary-Jo Jordan is quite poorly. They'll be there, I'm sure."

"I'll book the first flight I can for today, if possible. While I'm doing that, can you call Mrs. Fairman?" Sam took out his cell and sent Frankie her number.

They caught a midday flight from Fort Myers, and an hour and a half later, they were once again picking up a rental at Atlanta for the drive out to Sweet Clover Farm. Frankie drove.

"So, Mrs. Fairman had had no recent contact from Billy?"

"Not for quite a few weeks, she claims, but she said she wasn't worried, he wasn't in touch that regularly, anyway."

"Hmm, no real way of knowing if she's telling the truth, though. Okay, well, let's see what Mary-Jo and Gerald have to say."

It was late afternoon when they arrived at Sweet Clover Farm. Sam got out and used the gate phone.

"What now? Asked a weary sounding Gerald Jordan."

"We've got a development, and even if you're not interested, maybe your wife will be."

"She ain't too well."

"I'm really sorry to hear that, Mr. Jordan. Are you going to let us in? If not, it might be the cops come calling next time?" Sam heard Mary-Jo's voice in the background asking who was on the phone. There was a muffled exchange of words, then the gate slowly opened. Sam got back in the car, and they drove up to the farmhouse.

Gerald let them in with his usual ill grace and walked in front of them to the living room. Mrs. Jordan lay on her sofa. She looked much older today.

"Sit down, gentlemen. I heard the word, developments." Gerald looked grim. He knows, thought Frankie.

"I'll keep it short and to the point, Mrs. Jordan. Turns out that Gerald's son Clive is the Director in charge of the filming of Ricky's latest movie down in Naples."

"Yes, I know," said Mrs. Jordan, "he told me yesterday. Told me Clive had contacted him to say he was in trouble, that he'd been arrested." Sam looked directly at Gerald Jordan.

"And you knew about this how?"

"Clive's lawyer called me, said he might need my help to get a bond. Clive had been trying to get hold of someone else to sort it out, but hadn't been able to contact them. The lawyer said Clive was panicking and wanted out of jail." Sam turned to Mary-Jo,

"So, you had no idea before yesterday that Gerald's son was working closely with your son Ricky?"

"No, until yesterday, I didn't even know he had a son." She glared at Gerald Jordan, who'd found something interesting to look at on the floor. "Gerald told me," she continued, "and told me he'd got Clive the job with Ricky. All this went on behind my back and despite my calm exterior, I'm mad as hell at being kept in the dark." She stopped talking and took a sip of water from a beaker on the table.

"Clive was doing okay, Gerald says, but couldn't get any further with the production company he was working for and got in touch with his father, asked if he could put a word in with Ricky. Gerald and Ricky didn't always see eye to eye, but Gerald had a word with Ricky and knew he could rely on Ricky's good nature to help get Clive involved. Gerald told Ricky he thought it would be best if I didn't know." Sam thanked Mary-Jo then turned to Gerald Jordan and took out his notebook and pen.

"I have a question for you, Mr. Jordan. Where were you on Monday, October fifth?"

"Why do you want to know?"

"I think you can figure that out. So, I repeat, where were you on October fifth?" Gerald Jordan looked hesitant. "Look," Sam said, "You either provide us with an answer now, or the cops later, up to you."

"He was here, detective," said Mary-Jo. "All day. I know because that was the day we had a problem with one of the wells, and a maintenance crew had to come to fix it. Gerald was needed by the crew for various operational reasons to attend and spent all day with them. It was a long day and I remember Gerald being exhausted, having a long bath, a light supper and going to bed early."

"You're sure about that Mrs. Jordan?"

"I'm positive, yes. I suppose you could always check with the maintenance company, they'd be able to confirm it, I guess."

"Okay, well down the line, we might just do that. Another question Mr. Jordan. Did you sic Mr. Clarke on to me after I'd been to see Louise Fairman?" Jordan seemed to be weighing up his response. He looked uncomfortable, then spoke.

"No, the only person I told was Clive, I said you'd been here nosing around. He'd told me you'd been hired to look into this Billy's death, well, murder I suppose." Sam looked at Frankie, who said.

"Hang on. If, as seems likely, it was Clive who was then in contact with Bentley, how did Clive know about him?"

"Well, I...," Gerald stopped talking. There was a moment's silence, then Mary-Jo spoke, her voice increasing in volume...

"You told him the whole thing Gerald, didn't you?" said Mary-Jo. Gerald didn't reply "You stupid man," Mary-Jo yelled, "you stupid stupid man." Despite her frailty, her voice was forceful, her face red with rage. The silence in the room was deafening. Frankie spoke.

"So, Clive was in contact with Bentley, feeding information on to him. That all makes sense now." Sam nodded and looked at Gerald Jordan.

"Did you know Clive was in touch with Bentley?"

"No, I didn't., I swear."

"But you'd already told him the story about Mr. Clarke and the farm?"

"I've already... yes, I did."

"And did Clive know about Mr. Clarke and who he really was?" Gerald looked at Mary-Jo and hung his head, then looked up at Frankie.

"Shit, I knew that kid was no good. He's his mother's son alright"

"Could explain a lot," said Frankie, looking at Sam. Sam nodded. Gerald stood up

"I'm sorry Mary Jo," said Gerald, his sincerity seemed genuine. He went over to sit on the edge of the Mary-Jo's chair. Sam looked at Frankie, a quizzical look on his face, and spoke.

"We're just going outside for a few minutes. We'll leave the door open so we can get back in, okay?" Gerald Jordan nodded. Frankie and Sam walked out of the room, down the hall and out the front door.

"Well, what do you make of all that, Frankie boy?"

"In some ways, not a good fit with Gerald being involved in a conspiracy to kill Ricky, if it was Ricky who died, that is? I just don't know. Seems the more we find out, the more confusing it all gets. Maybe he was acting, trying to deflect?"

"Is it possible Clive and Billy cooked the inheritance thing up between just the two of them?"

"It's possible, but how could they get away with it long term? Gerald might be fooled for a short whole, but sure as hell, he'd soon realize Ricky wasn't really Ricky, Habits, shared memories and stuff like that. You can look like someone and sound like them, but you just wouldn't get away with it with someone who knew you intimately. Gerald helped bring Ricky up from being a baby."

"You're right. So, all that back there was just clever BS to put us off the scent, and maybe Gerald's up to his neck in it. Also, seems to me Clive just wouldn't have the imagination or the smarts. We obviously don't know Billy, so hard to judge. But then, maybe we do know Billy if we're right about Ricky possibly not being Ricky, and the motive."

"And another thing," said Sam, "I've just remembered about switching the DNA sample. He obviously knew about that, so how could he not be involved?"

"Good point. But even if we are right, as seems likely, then is there someone else pulling the strings? Someone very ambitious, very smart, and ruthless?"

"Look Frankie, all this speculation is driving us both mad and getting us nowhere. So, before we make any more guesses, we've got to have confirmation of the fingerprints. We're making all sorts of assumptions based purely on guesswork, ifs and maybes. I'll Call Captain Reagan see if he's made any progress." Sam took out his cell and was about to call. "No signal. I'll walk down to the gate, see if it improves." He came back a few minutes later.

"Alex has been trying to call me. He's got the results of Clive's gun. It's a legally held firearm, so nowhere to go with that. However, he's also got the prints from the autopsy for the body, and the prints from Ricky's DUI arrest."

"And?"

"We were right, they're a match to those from the autopsy. Looks like the dead guy we found wasn't Billy Fairman, it was Ricky Jordan."

"Holy shit!" Frankie thought about the implications for a minute. "What do we tell Mrs. Jordan? I can't imagine what effect it will have on her, especially as she's so sick... But we can't not tell her, can we?"

"I don't think it's our part to do that, I think we have to leave that to Captain Reagan and the authorities. There's a way to go yet."

"But Gerald Jordan's definitely a suspect. In the conspiracy, even if not directly involved in the murder, I mean?"

"Looks like it. Can't see how he's not involved, can you? Taking everything into account makes him a good fit."

"Do we need to do anything, now we know what we know?"

"No, not yet, we need to find out more. And anyway, Jordan ain't going anywhere. And there's always the outside possibility that we're wrong, although I'll eat my hat twice if we are."

CHAPTER 34

They caught the last flight from Atlanta, landing back in Fort Myers at 9:15 p.m. Traffic was light as they drove south along the I-75, both men deep in thought, reflecting on all they'd discovered. Sam's cell buzzed. He looked at the number and put the cell to his ear.

"Ross, let me put you on speaker, I'm with Frankie, in the car driving back from Fort Myers. We're just back from talking some more to the Jordans, hold on," Sam pressed the speaker symbol. Ross Shakey's voice came through loud and tinny but clear.

"Sorry I couldn't get back to you after we last spoke. I've been dashing around the country, meetings everywhere. I'm back in Naples now, and this is the first proper opportunity I've had to call you. Sounds like you've made progress and a lot has happened."

"It has Ross, yeah. Better if I call you when we get back to Frankie's condo. The signal fluctuates while we're moving."

"No, don't call me later, let's meet tomorrow and you can tell me the whole sorry saga. Sounds like you've been busy. I've rented a condo in Naples for a few days. I'm hoping I can combine some business with pleasure, maybe get some pool time and some sunbathing done on those fabulous Gulf beaches. I'll text you the address details. Say about 11:00 tomorrow, how does that sound?" Sam looked at Frankie, who shrugged his shoulders.

"Yeah, that suits us fine Ross, see you then," and he finished the call.

"She sounds happy," Frankie said.

"She does at that. How about I pick you up at 10:15 tomorrow?"

"I'll be ready."

Frankie woke up and went through his stretching routine on his lanai, then took Charlie for his jog come walk around venetian bay. Back in his condo, he fed Charlie, showered, then breakfasted. He checked the time, then went through his emails, replying where required and finally read the online UK newspapers, sipping his coffee.

A text on his cell arrived to tell him Sam was outside waiting. He donned a lightweight off-white linen jacket over a light blue T-shirt, dark blue chinos and brown leather loafers. He checked everything, and his appearance in the mirror, very respectable, then patted Charlie on the head, left the condo and walked down the stairs to the parking lot.

"Looking very smart today Frankie," said Sam, as Frankie got in the passenger seat.

"One has one's standards," he replied. Sam laughed and drove off to their appointment with Ross Sharkey. As they drove along, Sam asked.

"Did you have any thoughts about who the mastermind is?"

"I did have some, yes." They pulled up outside Palm Tree Court at 10:50 a.m. and got out of the car and made their way to the back of the complex. The ground floor unit Ross Sharkey had rented was situated on the west side of Venetian Bay, with its own private swimming pool on the back lawn and its own boat on a boat dock lift. Frankie looked at Sam.

"This lady rents in style," said Frankie. Sam pressed the bell. The door opened. Ross Sharkey opened the door, greeted them and waved them in.

"I've got a fresh pot of coffee on the go. Just sit yourselves down at the dining table and I'll bring it over, then you can help yourselves." The dining table was set with coffee cups for three. Sam and Frankie sat on either side of the table, leaving the place at the head of the table for Ross. She brought the coffee in on a fancy tray, along with a jug of cream and a bowl of sugar lumps.

"Just help yourselves gentlemen," setting it down in front of them. Frankie poured the coffee. When they were all settled, Sam began to tell the story, occasionally referring to his notes. Ross Sharkey listened patiently. Frankie interjected once or twice to explain the logic behind some of their questions. Sam carried on with his account of what had transpired during their investigations, Ross Sharkey occasionally gasping in shock, particularly when Sam said they'd found fingerprint evidence that made it almost certain that it was Ricky's dead body they'd found and not Billy Fairman's.

"No, that can't be. Are you positive, I mean, how could that possibly be? I knew Ricky better than I knew Billy, but surely, I'd have known. If what you say is true, then Billy is a truly stupendous actor. He certainly managed to fool me." Sam waited to resume his story. "Sorry to interrupt you Sam," said Ross, "please carry on." Sam continued and got to the part where Clive pulled a gun on him and Frankie, and once again, Ross expressed disbelief. "I haven't been able to get hold of Clive, so now I know why. This is terrible." Sam carried on telling her about their visit to the Jordan's the previous day and some of their conclusions.

"So, that's more or less it," Sam said and sat back.

"My God, I mean... all this going on underneath my nose. It's quite incredible." Then she put her elbows on the table and held her head in her hands a while, then looked up at Sam and Frankie.

"As you can imagine, I'm really finding it hard to process all this.... So, will arrests be made, I mean, where does it go from here?" Frankie spoke.

"We still think there's more to this Ross. We think there's someone else pulling the strings."

Suddenly the door opened, and Billy Fairman walked in holding a gun, a Ruger 4, Frankie thought. It was fitted with a suppressor.

"Hands flat on the table gents, now!" Sam and Frankie put their hands flat on the table.

Ross Sharkey looked genuinely surprised.

"Billy what the hell are you doing?"

"I heard enough. These guys have it all figured out, is my guess. All this, this, this story telling...it's bullshit, a charade. They're just pulling your chain Ross, wise up." Ross Sharkey looked at Sam. He smiled. Ross Sharkey stood up.

"You bastards!' she said. "Making a fool of me is very dangerous, as you'll find out." She turned to Billy. "And there was me thinking I was a great actress." Billy spoke without taking his attention from Sam and Frankie, continuously pointing the gun at one, then the other.

"Actor," said Billy, "no one says actress anymore. And no, you're not a good actor Ross."

"Fuck you Billy Fairman," she said. Billy smiled,

"Careful Ross" he said.

"Sorry Ricky, I didn't..., What do we do now?"

"Move well away from the table Ross, over to the right. Keep well away." She obeyed, moved away, and leaned against the wall. Billy moved slowly, keeping his gun pointed at both men, positioning himself a few feet behind Sam's back. He now had the back of Sam and the front of Frankie lined up in his sights.

"Now Sam, stand up, nice and easy. Take your jacket off slowly and throw it on the floor to your right." Sam complied, "Now, slowly take your gun out of its holster, put it on the table and slide it all the way to the right." Sam did as he was told. The gun skidded off the end of the table and on to the floor. Now, do the same with your cell phone" Sam took his cell phone out of his trousers pocket and slid it off the table. Billy moved to Sam's back and stuck the gun between his shoulder blades, then looking over Sam's shoulder at Frankie, he said

"Okay, same for you Frankie, but all to the left, okay? Frankie took off his jacket and threw it on the floor to his left, then removed his gun from its holster, put it on the table and slid it left. It too fell off the end and clattered on to the floor. He reached into his trouser pocket for his cell phone, "Slowly now," said Billy. Frankie nodded, then as he took his cellphone out, he fumbled, and the phone dropped to the floor.

"Oops," he said, and bent down to retrieve it.

"Leave it there," said Billy.

Frankie stood up, the Sig P365 ankle holster gun in his hand. Just as Billy realized what was happening, Frankie shot him three times in quick succession in his middle mass. Ross Sharkey screamed. Billy dropped to the floor like a stone

"Son of a bitch Frankie...! You kept that quiet," Sam said, as got up and went over to examine Billy's prone body. He kneeled down and felt for a pulse. "He's gone." said Sam. "Bentley's ankle gun?"

"Yeah, didn't want to spoil the surprise," Frankie replied, smiling. "Been practicing." Then he pocketed the 365, bent down to retrieve his cell and went to get his other gun off the floor. Sam collected his.

"You think anyone heard those shots, Sam?"

"I doubt it, sounded more like a pop gun." Sam turned to Ross who hadn't moved and seemed to be in a state of shock.

"Now, young lady, come over here and sit down. You have some questions to answer." Her face became stern and defiant. She folded her arms and still leaned against the wall.

"I'm not answering any questions, I want a lawyer." Sam smiled and nodded sideways for Frankie to go and get her. Frankie manhandled her over to the table and sat her down. Sam leaned over and stuck his face into hers. He spoke slowly and menacingly.

"You're mistaking this for a formal police interview, Ms. Sharkey. You don't have any rights in here, in fact, we might still decide to shoot you if you don't answer our questions. We'd have every justification." She shrugged in submission, then started to cry. "That won't work either, in fact, it's really annoying me." She stopped crying.

"Fuck you." She said with venom. Frankie came over and placed his cell phone on the table, looked at Sam and waited to press the record button.

"You seem to have a limited vocabulary when it comes to insults Ross. Now answer the questions and if we think you're telling the truth, you might get to live, understand?"

"Yes," she said grudgingly. Sam nodded at Frankie to start recording.

"Okay, I mentioned the fingerprint issue, but you didn't ask how they were relevant, because you already knew about it, and for that matter, everything else. You feigned surprise, but it wasn't convincing. Like Billy said, you're a crap actor Ross. So, who told you?" Ross Sharkey remained stock still. The defiant look had returned.

"Okay. Frankie, turn off the recording and pass me a cushion off that sofa." Frankie did as he asked.

"What are you doing?" asked Ross.

"The cushion will muffle the sound of the shot." Ross looked at him in horror. "Second thoughts Frankie, let's use Billy's gun, it has a silencer on it, and it seems sorta right, sort of poetic justice. Yeah, I like that. We can wipe the gun, then put Billy's prints back on the handle and blame him." Frankie retrieved Billy's gun and handed it to Sam. He put it to Ross's head. She squeezed her eyes shut and made a low wailing noise. Sam took the gun away. "Hang on, I need to shoot her from a few feet away, no point in going down for murder for the sake of thinking this through."

By now, Ross was whimpering. "Sorry Ross, were you trying to say something?" said Sam. "Now take a deep breath and talk to me. If you tell me the truth, who knows, you just might get to live, okay?" Ross nodded her head vigorously. Frankie pressed record again. "Right," said Sam, "how many of you were involved in the scam to get your hands on that farm, and who dreamed up the plan?"

"Billy. It was Billy. He was pissed at being poor all his life. Somehow, he found out Ricky was his blood brother. I was telling the truth when I said we employed him because they looked so much alike. It never occurred to us they were brothers until Billy told us."

"How did Billy know they were brothers?"

"When we first interviewed him for the role, he told us he'd always been a big fan of Ricky's ever since he saw Ricky's first movie. Said people used to remark on how alike they were. Sometimes, he said, he got mistaken for Ricky. Strangers would come up to him and ask for his autograph."

"Okay, but there must have been more."

"There was. After he came to work as Ricky's double, he became more and more convinced they were related. Seems he did some research on DNA and managed to get a DNA sample from Ricky's dressing room, and got it tested against his. He told us that the results confirmed that not only was he closely related to Ricky, but as the samples were an exact match, said that meant he had to be Ricky's twin brother."

"When you say he told us, who did he tell all this to exactly?"

"Initially, me and Clive, then later Clive talked to his father and got him involved. Gerald was another one with a grudge. Being denied any ownership of the farm. He resented Ricky being the sole beneficiary when his wife died. She's seriously ill now, so he knew it wouldn't be long before Ricky was the new owner. I don't think Ricky and his stepfather got on. Gerald felt he deserved to have it left to him, not Ricky. Billy's plan gave him the opportunity for the next best thing, significant part ownership."

"Anyone else?"

"No."

"You got any questions?" said Sam, turning to Frankie.

"Yes, I have. When Billy found out he had the same DNA as Ricky, didn't he ask his mother about it? Surely, he'd have asked her how that could be, or maybe he knew he was adopted."

"I asked him the same question," said Ross Sharkey.

"And?" said Frankie

"He told me to mind my own business where his mother was concerned. He was obviously very protective of his mother, or stepmother, whatever. So, I never got a clear answer."

"Okay," said Sam. "And where's Clive now?" Ross gave a little laugh.

"Where you were going to be, if, if things had gone to plan. He came to see us when he was released from jail. Billy thought he was a weak link and rather than have him interrogated by the cops, he killed him, then took his body out in the boat last night, weighted it down and dumped it in the middle of the bay."

"Jesus Christ Almighty," said Sam, shaking his head. He was silent for a while, letting it all sink in, then said, "By the way, smart move to employ us instead of letting us do our own thing." Ross Sharkey pulled a face. "What?" said Sam.

"I thought so too at the time, but it kinda backfired."

"How so?" Silence. "Come on Ross, the game's up. You might as well tell us the lot. If you're cooperative, it will go better for you. The more compliant you are, the better it's going to be for you in the end, so...?" She was silent for a few more moments, weighing up her situation.

"Okay, like you said, employing you meant I'd get updates on anything you found out. Not that we expected you to find out much. But Clive told his father that you'd likely be going to see Mrs. Fairman. So, Gerald Jordan, in turn, alerted Mr. Clarke, or whatever his name is. Mr. Clarke is a little paranoid, it seems, and asked someone to arrange to keep an eye on Mrs. Fairman for a few days.

When you turned up, it was expected, but then when you then followed her afterwards..., Clive said they got rattled, thought you might have discovered more than you should."

"So, they kidnapped and interrogated me to make sure."

"Yes. A Mr. Bentley, something to do with the FBI, he put two guys on it. I understand they were supposed to kill you afterwards, regardless of you knowing anything or not. Seems Clarke wanted to eliminate you as a threat, remove any possibility of you finding anything out. Especially as he suspected the kidnapping itself would make you think there was a more going on. That's as much as I know."

"Okay," said Sam, "now we come to the sixty-four-thousand-dollar question, who killed Ricky Jordan?" Ross hesitated, then said.

"Billy. Billy Fairman shot him. Billy's a killer. He killed Clive, and you know he was going to kill you."

"Hmm, what do you think Frankie, she telling the truth?"

"I'm not really sure Sam. The other two prime suspects are conveniently dead, so she could claim it was either Clive or Billy. Thing is, Ricky was shot with a .22 and somehow, it doesn't seem a good fit for Billy."

"Yeah, I agree," said Sam, looking at Billy's gun, which he still held in his hand. "This ain't no .22 caliber."

"I have a suggestion," said Frankie, "why don't we look in this lady's purse, see if she owns such a gun?" Ross Sharkey looked stricken. "No, that's private property, don't you dare!" Frankie wandered over to the couch where Ross had left her purse. He picked it up and rummaged inside and brought out a small handgun. Frankie looked it over, "A Bernardelli Baby pistol, a very neat little gun. I'd say that might probably prove to be the gun that killed poor old Ricky."

"I think you could well be right Frankie. Anything you want to say Ross?"

"Fuck you both," she said.

"How did I know you were going to say that?" said Sam, then he and Frankie both burst into laughter. When they'd recovered their composure, Sam asked.

"You think we have enough here Frankie?"

"I think so," said Frankie, picking his cell phone up off the table.

"Hey, hold on there," said Ross, "you can't use that recording against me. Whatever I said was clearly said under duress, you haven't got a prayer of convicting me on that shit."

"Maybe not, we'll leave that to the legal guys. Got to say, though, I'm still tempted to shoot you here and now, save everyone a lot of time and trouble. Whaddya think Frankie?"

"It's tempting, but I think I'd rather see her turn turtle on Gerald Jordan, don't you?"

"Good point Frankie boy. Let's call Reagan. He'll need to get his CS boys down here and formally arrest Ms. Sharkey here."

CHAPTER 35

Ross Sharkey and Gerald Jordan were arrested and charged, but both let out on bail. The gun they'd taken off Ross Sharkey was found to be the one used in the shooting and murder of Ricky Jordan. Clive Susman's body was recovered by frogmen from Venetian Bay. The gun belonging to Billy Fairman proved to be the one that killed Susman.

Charges for Ross Sharkey included Murder one. Other charges for both included conspiracy to Commit Murder, conspiracy to Commit Fraud, and various associated criminal charges. Sadly, the revelations exposed in the affair dealt a serious blow to Mary-Jo Jordan's already failing health. As a result, she had to leave the farm for a hospice, so she could spend her last days being cared for in relatively pain-free comfort.

Frankie and Sam went to visit Mary-Jo in the hospice to bring her up to date with developments. She was grateful to them for exposing her husband for the man he really was.

"Gerald was always an angry man. I don't think he was ever happy with his lot. He had everything, but never seemed satisfied. Ironically, with Ricky and Billy gone, I would probably have left the farm to him. Now he gets nothing, well, other than a long spell in jail, which he thoroughly deserves."

"You may not be willing to say, Mrs. Jordan," said Frankie, "but will you tell us who Mr. Clarke really is?" Mary-Jo thought for a moment, then gestured for them both to come closer.

"Closer," she said, and revealed the identity of the man known to them as Mr. Clarke. "I'm tired now. I need to sleep," Mary-Jo said and closed her eyes. Frankie and Sam left. A few days later they were informed that Mary-Jo Jordan had passed away peacefully in her sleep, the night following their visit.

A further week went by, then Sam received a phone call from Martinson & Blackwell, lawyers in Atlanta. After a few security questions to establish his identity, the lawyer, Bertram Blackwell, informed Sam that there was a package on its way to him by courier and he should receive it the following day. Mrs. Jordan had asked Blackwell to tell Sam to handle the contents with discretion.

"Tell me, Mr. Blackwell, what's going to happen to the farm now?"

"Mrs. Jordan changed her will. Her new instructions are to sell the farm and to donate most of the proceeds to a number of charities comprising mainly of orphanages and charities that help unmarried mothers. She gave very specific instructions that we check the worthiness of any of these institutions before releasing any funds to them. There'll be plenty of money to go round, that farm is worth a huge amount of money."

"You said 'most of the proceeds," Sam said.

"Yes, a sizable chunk goes to an individual.

"I assume you can't reveal who that individual is?"

"Mrs. Jordan's instructions were clear. The identity of that individual is confidential."

"I understand," said Sam. He thanked Mr. Blackwell, rang off, and called Frankie. He repeated details of the conversation he'd just had with Blackwell.

"So, who do you think the mystery beneficiary is?"

"If there's any justice in this world, it would be Louise Fairman."

"That would be my guess too. I assume the package Mary-Jo's sending you will be the incriminating tape or film. If it is, do we check it out or just assume it is what we think it is?"

"I don't want to speculate. Let's see what it is first, but if it's the film, then yes, we have to make sure."

"I suppose we do, said Frankie grimacing. But being filmed on such old equipment, how are we going to see what's on it?"

"Let's see what it is first, then I can ask around at the station. I know they have third party resources to look at old films and stuff if necessary. They find all sorts of odd evidence when they're investigating cold cases."

"Okay, but it turns my stomach to think about watching it. Especially as we now know who the guy is. You couldn't get a self-righteous and pious individual if you tried."

"Ain't it always the way Frankie? The pious ones are the worst."

CHAPTER 36

The following day, a courier delivered the package to Sam's home. He called Frankie and told him it had arrived.

"What does it look like?"

"Like a plastic cassette."

"Was there anything with it, a note or anything?"

"Just a brief note that said, *I hope this will help keep you safe. Thanks for all your help, Mary-Jo.*"

"Okay so what next?"

"I enquired with the department that handles cold cases and they've put me on to a guy they've used in the past. A movie buff called Cyril Mathews, really knows his stuff and trustworthy, they say. Apparently, there's quite a few enthusiasts who collect vintage movie equipment. They even get together to arrange movie nights and watch old movies on old equipment. No accounting for what some folks are interested in. I've got his number, so I'll call him and see if he can help." Sam called back an hour later to say Cyril said it shouldn't be a problem and they should go to his house the following night at 8:00 p.m.

Cyril lived on Devil's Bight, just off Crayton Road. They arrived early. Cyril welcomed them into his house. Seems normal enough, thought Frankie. Cyril offered them a drink or coffee, but they declined the offer, eager to get on with the task in hand. They were escorted out of the rear of the house into a spacious back yard where a separate substantial wooden building stood.

On the way over, they'd discussed once again if it was necessary to see what was on the tape, both of them not relishing the prospect of watching it, but they both felt they had no choice. Cyril opened the door, and they went in. There was equipment everywhere, all neatly stacked on shelves. There was a mini cinema in the form of six chairs facing the back of the room. Cyril asked for the film cassette and smiled in recognition,

"Shouldn't be a problem," he said, and indicated they should sit. He took a projector off one of the shelves, placed it on a pedestal, and plugged it into a wall socket. Then he went to the back wall of the room and pulled down a white screen. Going back to the projector, he switched it on, and a light shone on the screen. He inserted the cassette, checked some of the controls, then spoke.

"Let me show you how to start this thing." Sam stood and went to stand next to him. "It's quite simple, just flick that switch down there, and it should all start to happen. You can let it run until it runs out of road, or switch off by flicking it to the up position, okay? I'll switch the big light off on the way out. It's just by the door if you need the lights back on. Be in the house if you need me, okay?" Sam waited till he'd left and stood by the projector.

"You ready Frankie?"

"As ready as I'll ever be." Frankie winced as Sam flicked the switch. Some flickering black and white symbols came up, then the screen went blank, then gray, then some images appeared on the screen, accompanied by music. Tom and Jerry appeared and proceeded to chase each other round a kitchen. Frankie turned to Sam, who looked back at Frankie.

"Well, I'll be... Son of a bitch!" said Sam, a look of total disbelief on his face, "we need to see if that's all there is. I'll go get Cyril, see if we can speed this thing up so we can watch it all." Cyril came and showed them how to turn a knob that controlled the speed, then left them to get on with watching the rest of the film. They watched the rest of Tom

& Jerry at speed. Then there was a break for a few seconds. Both men tensed as the film changed, then a Road Runner cartoon started to play.

"Jesus Christ," said Frankie. Sam shook his head. They let it run to the end, then found Cyril, thanked him and left, taking the cartoon film with them. They got into Sam's car. Sam hit the steering wheel hard with his hand, threw the cassette on the rear seat, then drove off, tires screeching. He slowed down eventually and spoke.

"We need to go see Gerald Jordan, find out what the hell's going on."

CHAPTER 37

A couple of days later, Frankie returned from his usual morning jog with Charlie, then completed the rest of his morning routine before sitting down in front of his PC to catch up on his emails and check the news.

When he was done, he checked the time and wondered if Sam had yet had the chance to speak with Cap Reagan about going to see Gerald Jordan while he was in custody. He called Sam's cell. He didn't answer, so he left a voicemail message.

Sam rang back ten minutes later.

"Got your message and yes, I've spoken to Reagan. Frankie, you won't believe this."

"Try me."

"Jordan and Sharkey have walked, as in not going to be prosecuted."

"What?!"

"Afraid so," Sam went on to tell Frankie that Ross Sharkey claimed the gun they'd found in her purse was Billy's. Swore that Billy told her to keep it for him. And she did as he asked because she was terrified of him. "The gun did have both her and Billy's prints on it.

"Her attorney argued successfully that there was no real evidence to suggest her story wasn't true. And furthermore, it had been established that Billy was a killer. That all the evidence pointed at Billy Fairman. Ross Sharkey claimed Billy killed Ricky Jordan, and Clive Susman."

"And the prosecutor bought that? What about the tape?"

"Inadmissible as Sharkey had predicted."

"So, she goes free?"

"Yup, and not only that, but she also claims she doesn't know Gerald Jordan at all. Says she thinks she heard Clive and Billy talking about him once."

"Jesus Christ. What about Gerald Jordan, are we allowed to go and see him?"

"Only if he agrees. See, he's off the hook as well." Frankie slumped in his chair. "You still there Frankie?"

"Yes, just trying to process all this. How?"

"No one to provide any evidence against him. Sharkey couldn't, without implicating herself, and everyone else is dead. Apart from us, and what can we prove?"

"Lord above. Do you think Jordan will agree to see us?"

"He might. Depends how secure he feels. Might want to gloat, you just never know with guys like him. I'll think about how to approach it and maybe call him later."

Sam Called Gerald Jordan later that day. The Jordan's house phone was answered by a new voice.

"Hold on," the voice said, then Sam heard her shout, "Gerry honey, there's a Mr. Rindozzo on the phone wanting to speak with you." *that didn't take him long*, Thought Sam.

"Okay honey," said the distant voice, "coming." Sam heard footsteps, then Jordan took the phone.

"What do you want?"

"We wanted to come and talk to you."

"I got nothing to say to you."

"Okay, but before you put the phone down, could you just answer one question?"

"Depends, try me, what's the question?" Sam thought he might as well get straight to the point."

"We went to see Mary-Jo in hospital."

"Yeah, I know, so?"

"She told us who Mr. Clarke is."

"Did she now. So now you know."

"She also sent us the film cassette." Gerald Jordan laughed derisively.

"You enjoy the cartoons? I like the Road Runner one best, don't you?"

"Very funny, I guess you have the original one."

"Yeah, I got the original one. Gives me some protection, but not that much now."

"How so?"

"Think about it deetective," Jordan said lengthening the word to express disdain for Sam's deductive powers, "as long as Mary-Jo was alive, the guy knew there was a witness who could provide the damning evidence, substantiate what the film showed. But now she's passed, he'll realize, at worst, it's just a dirty movie of an older guy having sex with a younger woman. Nothing to say who the girl was or what age she was. That the film exists might be kind of intimidating for him maybe, but without a witness, not so much anymore."

"I assume Mary-Jo thought she had the original film of her having sex with him?" Jordan laughed.

"Yeah, I switched it a while back. She's too soft hearted. I didn't know what she might do, she might have even destroyed the cassette. I wasn't sure, so I switched it. I knew without that film, the guy would kill me soon as...whatever."

"So even though he knows you still have the film...?"

"Yeah, I know. So, okay, it wouldn't do him any favors if it was released, but he wouldn't be in big trouble. He could just say it was an aberration. He didn't even know it was being filmed. He could claim she was of legal age. I don't know. What I do know is, I don't have the same level of insurance now that Mary-Jo's passed. And he might well decide to make sure I never blab." Sam couldn't think of an appropriate response, Gerald Jordan continued unprompted.

"So, I'm not taking any chances, I'm leaving. We're going to find somewhere in the sun to live, somewhere he won't find me. I'm well fixed. My stipend carries on even when the farm's sold. I'm gonna marry Kim, Miss Pennsylvania 2015. As pretty as hell, and a great piece of ass. Nice speaking with you detective. Give my best to your buddy." Jordan hung up the phone.

"Shit," said Sam and called Frankie and told him about the conversation. Frankie listened without interruption.

"Can't fault his logic. Looks like the Kevlar vests are going to be de rigueur until we figure out what to do about this."

"Yeah, maybe. Look, I'm going to call that lawyer, see if I can find out anything useful. Sam cut the line, looked for the call from Bertram Blackwell, and called the number. The receptionist told him Mr. Blackwell was busy on another line. Sam said he'd wait. After a few minutes, Blackwell came on the line. Sam introduced himself.

"Yes, I remember you Mr. Randazzo, what can I do for you? I assume you received the package, okay?"

"I did thanks. I'm calling about the farm. Is it still going to be sold, as you told me previously?"

"It's sold already. A pretty place like that with substantial oil reserves is a very attractive piece of real estate. They don't come much more attractive."

"Who bought it?"

"Oh, I'm not at liberty to say., but I can tell you it was a very wealthy Canadian gentleman, if that helps."

"And what happens to Gerald Jordan now? Mrs. Jordan told me there was an agreement in her will that any buyer of the farm would have to agree to continue to pay her husband a stipend. Does that remain in place?"

"Yes, it does. It was included as a condition of the sale. The new owner must abide by that agreement. Why do you ask?"

"Just curious."

A few weeks later, news reports started to appear in the media about the release of the late Ricky Jordan's new block buster movie Backlash. It was all the more sensational due to the previously shocking headline news, that while making the movie, Ricky Jordan had been shot to death - gunned down by his own estranged twin brother.

If that wasn't enough, the story became even more sensational, when it was revealed that in the latter part of the movie, Ricky Jordan was played by Billy Fairman, twin brother and killer of Ricky Jordan. The media and the public couldn't get enough of it.

Further reporting told the story of how Billy Fairman was subsequently shot and killed by private detectives looking into the original murder. The news channels went ballistic, as did social media.

Sam and Frankie were identified by the media, as the private investigators who were involved in the shooting of Billy Fairman. They were subsequently plagued by journalists, radio and TV and chat shows, to give their account of what happened. They declined all offers, sometimes with difficulty considering the financial incentives on offer.

TV coverage invariably included pictures of Ross Sharkey, rubbing shoulders with the Hollywood glitterati, as she too became an overnight sensation. Interviewed on every TV channel and radio station that could get her. She invariably blubbed about the tragic loss of a truly fine actor in such violent circumstances. Especially for such a gentle soul, etc. etc. The public lapped it up, and it became obvious to Sam and Frankie that she'd soon become an extremely wealthy and celebrated individual.

Predictably, the movie sold out in every cinema showing it. Extra performances had to be scheduled to keep up with demand. The term 'blockbuster' was hardly sufficient to describe it, and commentators struggled to find more and more extreme superlatives to describe its runaway success.

Sam and Frankie went on with their lives. Business was good after all the publicity and it kept their minds occupied, but they often discussed Mr. Clarke. They still referred to him by that name despite knowing he was in fact, US senator, Clarence Martyn Murphy-O'Connor.

When they'd first discovered his real identity, Frankie did some research and found an old newspaper article on the senator in the New York Times.

'US senator, Clarence Martyn Murphy-O'Connor is much admired for his wit and oratory, and skills of persuasion. He is known as Marty O'Connor to his friends and 'Smart Mart' to his adversaries, as, it's claimed, he always seemed to be one step ahead of everyone else.' The article went on to list his achievements and finished by saying that O'Connor had married in his late thirties to Boston socialite Mary Appleton, but the marriage didn't last and ended in divorce after five years. There were no children.

CHAPTER 38

Some time later, events took place that changed everything. The first was the tragic news that Ross Sharkey, the accomplished movie producer, attributed with the success of the internationally acclaimed smash hit movie, Backlash, predicted to sweep all before it at next year's Academy Awards and the Emmys, had died tragically in a hit-and-run incident in Los Angeles. The driver involved had fled the scene and was never found.

The second event attracted hardly any publicity and was only brought to Frankie and Sam's attention by Captain Reagan. Frankie searched for more news on Google and found a report posted by AP. He emailed the link on to Sam. The article said, 'Gerald Jordan, originally from Florida, and his recently wed bride, Kim Jordan, died whilst snorkeling off the coast of Barbuda, where the couple had recently bought a home. Initial reports indicated the couple ran out of air during a dive on a sunken ship. The authorities are investigating but stated that foul play is not suspected at this stage.'

The article went on to quote statistics on how many divers, lose their lives in the United States and Canada every year due to scuba diving accidents.' After reading the report, Frankie called Sam.

"You read the stuff I just sent you on the Jordans?"

"Just."

"Senator Marty O'Connor tidying up d'you think?"

"More than that. My guess is its punishment, or revenge if you prefer. He probably considers Sharkey and Jordan responsible for the deaths of his two sons.

"Yes, I suppose they were really. But isn't O'Connor running the risk of that film being made public now? I mean now that Gerald Jordan has met, what you might call, an untimely death?"

"Depends on what arrangements Jordan made, but my guess is it won't. Gerald Jordan was right. Without May-Jo, there's no one to verify its authenticity or the incriminating details. Anything anyone else claims, is just hearsay at best.

"Anyway, I think our main concern now, should be how much of an ongoing threat O'Connor represents to us. He's proved he still has the reach, and the means to kill off anyone involved in the deaths of his sons."

"On that basis, I must be a prime target. After all, I'm the one who actually shot and killed Billy Fairman."

"Yeah, but my guess is O'Connor considers we both share the blame for that."

"You think?"

"I do. In fact, I was thinking about this the other night and checked out O'Connor's stance on law and order. He's a deluded hypocrite. An Old Testament bible thumper - tooth for a tooth, eye for an eye kinda guy - and that really worries me. His sons were both killed, and he probably thinks anyone involved has to pay accordingly."

"But he must know I had no choice. I only shot Billy in self-defense."

"Self-righteous people like O'Connor don't care about justification when it comes to their own. Believe me Frankie, I've had plenty of experience of people like him."

"So, what do we do?"

"I'm not sure. See I'm the one with kids." Frankie was silent for a beat.

"You're not saying he'd go after your kids?"

"I don't know Frankie, I just don't know. He's crazy enough. Regardless, he'll come after us two for sure. And it's all my fault. I got us into this. If I hadn't decided to get us involved, and left it to Reagan, we wouldn't be in this situation."

"You can't blame yourself Sam. I volunteered, you didn't talk me into it. Anyway, more importantly, what do we do about it?"

"I don't know, I'm thinking on it. But in the meantime, we're going to have to have eyes in the back of our heads."

The next event happened nearly two months later, when Senator Marty O'Connor became engulfed in a financial scandal that rocked Washington. A journalist exposed blatant insider trading, with allegations of confidential knowledge being used by certain senators, to buy or dump stock. The journalist claimed that O'Connor, in particular, was guilty of a clear violation of the Stock Act.

There were ongoing investigations and huge amounts of adverse publicity. Senator O'Connor's position became increasingly untenable.

He hadn't yet been found guilty in any formal way but was being called on to resign by many in the press - and even by members of his own party. There were a number of subsequent opinion pieces in the media on how 'O'Connor, a strident law and order campaigner, had brought public humiliation on himself and on the party he represented.' Frankie and Sam kept abreast of events.

"All very interesting," said Sam one evening as they'd finished talking business and were chatting about the senator.

"Maybe there is such a thing as poetic justice," said Frankie. "Senator O'Connor's star is obviously fading. Maybe he crossed someone more powerful than himself?"

"Seems likely. I wonder if he's lost his FBI connections. Looks to me like he's being thrown to the wolves."

Sam and Frankie continued to follow events which culminated a few weeks later with a statement from the Senator to the effect that he'd been 'the victim of a vicious witch hunt. That 'the allegations were false. But in the interests of The House, and the reputation of Government and his Party, he'd made the decision to spend some time at his hunting lodge in Montana, planning a strategy to clear his name and restore his reputation.' "I'll be back," the report quoted him as saying.

The following day, Sam and Frankie met to discuss their latest assignment. It involved a wealthy trader who suspected his partner of fraud. It wasn't an easy case, and involved a fair amount of research before starting to follow the guy to see what he was up to, who he met with etc. Research was much more Frankie's forte than Sam's. Sam much preferred the hands-on stuff.

They were sitting in Frankie's condo discussing some details and settled on a plan of action.

"You're not going to need me for a few days," said Sam, "so I'm going to take off for a short break, okay?"

"Sure thing."

"Be good if you could give me a lift to Fort Myers Airport tomorrow morning, if that's okay.?"

"Of course, Sam, no problem. You and Martha going anywhere nice?"

"No, not taking Martha, going with Lucas, an old buddy of mine. Thought I'd go and try some hunting and fishing, you know, something different."

"You, hunting and fishing. Are you kidding me?"

"No, I'm not kidding you. It's good to try new things. You can get into a rut you know. I'm not a bad shot with a rifle. Maybe not quite as good as you, but I'm pretty good. And anyone can use a fishing pole. You'll be okay without me for a while, won't you?"

"Oh, I think I'll manage." Frankie laughed. "Who would have thought?" He shook his head. "You booked a guide?"

"No, I thought I'd leave it till we get there."

"And where is there?"

"I heard Montana's good for that sort of thing, so I've booked a flight to Bozeman."

"Montana," Frankie nodded. "Interesting. You might need some warm clothes this time of year. And who's this buddy Lucas again? Never heard you mention him before."

"Old friend, we go way back." Sam took out a driver's license from his wallet and handed it to Frankie "This is him."

"Lucas Brigstock. Gosh, he looks a lot like you." He handed the license back.

"I know, people used to say we could be twins. So, can you pick me up at six thirty tomorrow morning? Got to get there a bit early to check the gun in as hold luggage."

"No problem."

The following morning, Frankie picked Sam up as arranged. Traffic was light as they drove to the airport. Frankie made small talk and told some of his dreadful jokes. They arrived at the airport entrance and Sam got out. Frankie jumped out, grabbed Sam's carryon bag and rifle case from the back of the jeep, and handed them to Sam. He wished his friend goodbye. They shook hands.

"Safe journey, Sam, and good hunting."

"Thanks Frankie, I'm confident I'll bag me a nice trophy."

"Make sure you do that Sam. I'm relying on you." And with that, Frankie got back in the jeep and drove away.

Two days later, Frankie's cell phone pinged. A text from Sam asking Frankie to pick him up at Fort Myers Airport at 5:15 p.m. Frankie parked up and went to the arrivals gate. He was a few minutes early and was passing the time of day talking to a porter when Sam came through the doors, carrying the gun case, his carryon bag over his shoulder. He saw Frankie and walked over to him.

"Welcome Back."

"Thanks Frankie, good to be back."

"Good trip?"

"Yeah, I guess." They walked towards the parking lot to collect Frankie's jeep.

"How did Lucas enjoy the trip?"

"Oh, he loved it. In fact, he liked Montana so much, he decided to stay."

"Really?" said Frankie,

"Yeah, I know. The guy was always a bit impulsive. Anyway, anything much happen while I was away?"

"Nothing I couldn't handle. There was some sensational news about Senator Murphy-O'Connor, though. Found dead in a ravine underneath the deck of his hunting lodge."

"Yeah, I heard about that, tragic."

"Lots of speculation in the media about how he died. Apparently, the ravine was directly under the deck of this hunting lodge. A three or five-hundred-foot drop, depending on who was telling the story. No gunshot or stab wounds, apparently. They say he either jumped or was pushed. The cops aren't saying what they think." Frankie looked at Sam, who shrugged and nodded.

"Got to be one or the other," he said. Frankie continued,

"Some were linking it to the financial scandal he was mired in and suggesting suicide, others, a home invasion gone wrong. What's your take on it, Sam?"

"Suicide probably. Seems to fit the circumstances. Loss of status, the embarrassment for a powerful guy like that, being caught with his hands in the cookie jar."

"A credible explanation," said Frankie, "he wouldn't be the first powerful guy to commit suicide due to loss of face." They got to his jeep. Frankie took Sam's bag and rifle case and put them in the back. Sam climbed into the passenger seat. Frankie drove out of the airport and joined the I-75 heading south towards Naples.

"By the way," said Sam, "are you and Daisy free this Friday evening, by any chance?"

"I think so, why?"

"I thought you might like to come to our place. My homemade cannelloni is legendary, nothing like the shop bought stuff, I promise. Martha loves a dinner party, especially when I do the cooking. And I've got some great Prosecco, some delicious Primitivo from Puglia, where my father's family comes from, and some Grappa that will knock your socks off."

"We'll be there. What are we celebrating?"

"Oh, I don't know, life, liberty, happiness, I guess."

"And justice?"

"Yeah, definitely justice."

———— ⟨∾⟩ ————

Dedications
For

For Joe Mainous, Capt. Dave Ramsey (Park Shore Marina) and all our dear friends at Orleans The Moorings, Naples

ACKNOWLEDGEMENTS
Lyn Costello
Jasia Painter
John Sansom
Brian Borgford
Zsolt Monostory

Message from the author

Thank you for reading Backlash. I hope you enjoyed it. If you did, I'd be very grateful if you would leave a review. Reviews are essential to the success of any book. And once again, thanks for reading my novel.

Best wishes
Kerry Costello

About the Author

Kerry Costello
Born in the UK but of Irish heritage, Costello has homes in both the UK and Naples Florida, the latter, he says, is a great source of material for his books.

https://www.kerrycostellobooks.com/

KERRY COSTELLO

By the same author

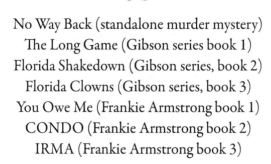

No Way Back (standalone murder mystery)
The Long Game (Gibson series book 1)
Florida Shakedown (Gibson series, book 2)
Florida Clowns (Gibson series, book 3)
You Owe Me (Frankie Armstrong book 1)
CONDO (Frankie Armstrong book 2)
IRMA (Frankie Armstrong book 3)

https://www.kerrycostellobooks.com/
Book video trailer
https://youtu.be/u7plOZDOB7A

Lightning Source UK Ltd.
Milton Keynes UK
UKHW040727170123
415494UK00004B/328